"Come on, let's go up to the house."

Somehow she had to get him to warmth and light and the shelter of four walls.

Awkwardly, because she was still clutching his sleeve, he stood upright. He was four or five inches taller than she. His body was shaking as if he had a fever.

"I don't know the way," he said in a low voice.

For a horrified moment Casey wondered if she was alone in the woods with a madman. "But you live here," she faltered. "We're not that far from the house."

The muscles clenched under her fingers. He said harshly, "I'm blind...hadn't you guessed? I must have looked like a fool, floundering around on all those rocks...a damned fool."

SANDRA FIELD, once a biology technician, now writes full-time under the pen names of Jocelyn Haley and Jan MacLean. She lives with her son in Canada's Maritimes, which she often uses as a setting for her books. She loves the independent life-style she has as a writer. She's her own boss, sets her own hours and increasingly there are travel opportunities.

Books by Sandra Field

Don't miss any of our special offers. Write to us at the following address for information on our newest releases.

Harlequin Reader Service
P.O. Box 1397, Buffalo, NY 14240
Canadian address: P.O. Box 603,
Fort Erie, Ont. L2A 5X3

SANDRA FIELD

love at first sight

Harlequin Books

TORONTO • NEW YORK • LONDON
AMSTERDAM • PARIS • SYDNEY • HAMBURG
STOCKHOLM • ATHENS • TOKYO • MILAN

My thanks to Meredith Ripley
of the Canadian National Institute
for the Blind,
Halifax, Nova Scotia.

A donation from the proceeds of this book
will be made to
Canadian Guide Dogs for the Blind,
Manotick, Ontario,
to whom I also express my appreciation.

Harlequin Presents first edition February 1991
ISBN 0-373-11336-6

Original hardcover edition published in 1990
by Mills & Boon Limited

LOVE AT FIRST SIGHT

PROLOGUE

'YOU'VE *what*?' Jenny Sibley demanded.

'I've rented the house out,' Bryden Moore repeated patiently.

'Whatever *for*?'

Before Bryden could reply, Jenny's husband interposed mildly, 'Jenny, darling, calm down.'

'I can't, I don't understand—what on *earth* are you renting the house out for, Bryden, you're not going anywhere, are you?' Unspoken in the air hung another question... how can you go anywhere now?

Bryden's hand tightened around his glass; the skin was pale, too pale considering the blazing sun that was knifing through the chinks in the bamboo blinds. But his voice, to all except those who knew him well, would have sounded normal and relaxed. 'Where do I always go in August?' he drawled. 'Got to get out of this Ottawa heat somehow.'

'You're going to the cottage?' Jenny squeaked. 'But——'

Her husband sent her a warning glance. 'Good idea,' he said. 'It's really been intolerable the last three weeks, hasn't it? The Oultons will be glad to leave as well, I'm sure.' The Oultons had looked after Bryden's house, which was next door to the Sibleys', for over five years.

Bryden carefully placed the glass on the solid teak coffee-table in front of him; it had been bought in Jenny's Scandinavian phase, while the bamboo blinds were a result of her trip to China. 'Look, let's not play

7

games,' he said roughly. 'The Oultons aren't going. I'm going alone.'

For once Jenny was struck dumb. Matthew Sibley, after a perceptible pause, said with the licence of a long friendship, 'Do you think that's wise, Bryden?'

'Maybe not. But that's what I'm doing.'

Jenny had had time to recover. 'You only go to the cottage for a month—so why are you renting the house out?'

'I'm staying for the winter.'

'For the winter? What about your job?'

'I've taken a year's leave of absence.'

Staring at him as if he had taken leave of his senses, she gasped, 'Have you fired the Oultons?'

'They'll stay next door. Part of the rental package.'

Matthew ran his fingers through his salt-and-pepper hair, his grey eyes concerned. 'I think this calls for another round of drinks,' he said heavily.

Jenny, less circumspect, leaned forward, a bar of sun glinting in her tumbled red curls. 'You *can't* stay alone, Bryden—it's impossible!'

'It's my sight I've lost, not my brains!' Bryden snapped. 'Stop treating me as if I'm mentally retarded.'

'I'm *not*. You're so intelligent you scare the life out of me, I can't even balance my budget while you deal with three-dimensional equations and research so abstract I don't even know how you put it down on something as mundane as paper. But you *are* blind, Bryden—you'll go crazy at Ragged Island on your own for a year!'

'I'll go crazy if I stay here.'

Bryden's voice had been devoid of emotion. But Jenny's vision suddenly blurred with tears, for she was a warm-hearted woman and could guess the sterility and pain that lay behind his words. Allowing her feelings to override caution, she rested her hand on Bryden's wrist, enveloping him in a wave of expensive perfume and feminine concern.

His recoil was instant, almost instinctive; she could have anticipated it, for she had known him a long time. She dropped his wrist and said incoherently, 'Oh, Bryden, I'm so *sorry* ...'

'You'll have another Scotch, Bryden?' Matthew said with ponderous tact.

'No, thanks. I'm meeting the rental agent in half an hour to sign the final papers; I'll have to be going.'

'You mean it isn't final yet?' Jenny asked, hope brightening her jade-green eyes.

'Jenny, I'm spending the next year at Ragged Island— that's final,' Bryden replied.

She ignored her husband's gesture towards her glass. 'You're running away,' she announced. 'You're going to bury yourself in the country and pretend——'

'Jenny!' Matthew exclaimed.

Bryden reached for his long white cane and got to his feet. 'I'm doing what I think is best,' he said tightly. Then he nodded in Matthew's direction. 'Thanks for the Chivas Regal, Matt, it sure beats the rest of them, doesn't it?'

He had long been familiar with the layout of the Sibleys' living-room. His movements unhurried, full of assurance, he crossed the room and headed for the front door. Jenny scurried after him. 'You're not cross with me, are you, Bryden?' she wailed. 'Please don't be!'

His face softened, his eyes the same smoke-blue they had always been. 'You're forgiven,' he said lightly. 'I won't be leaving for three or four days, you must both come over and have a drink before I go. Just as long as you don't try and make me change my mind.'

'No chance of that,' Jenny responded tartly. 'Although I could tell your rental agent that the neighbours are terrible.'

'I've already warned him,' was the bland reply. 'See you later.'

The oak door with its swirls of leaded glass, which dated from Jenny's Olde English period, closed behind him. Matthew said drily, 'You excelled yourself today, sweetheart.'

'Do you know what absolutely *kills* me?' she gulped, blinking back more tears and ignoring his statement. 'The way he uses words like look and see just as if he still can...Matthew, what are we going to *do*?'

'I'm going to give you a hug and take you out for lunch,' Matthew said promptly.

Jenny flung her arms around her husband's rather too considerable girth, her brow furrowed in thought. She adored Matthew, but did not consider him infallible. 'We can't just let him disappear into the wilds of Nova Scotia,' she mumbled. 'For a whole *year*.'

'Darling, Bryden is twenty-nine years old and has always been what you might call a man of strong will, to put it mildly. If he says he's going to spend the winter at the cottage, then he will. And who knows, it might be the best thing for him?'

Jenny raised her head. 'How can you even *think* that, let alone say it? He'll *die* of loneliness down there, Matthew. He *hates* being blind, and he's far too proud to ask for help, so he'll end up stuck in the house day after day, I know he will.'

'If he gets lonely enough, he'll do something about it. Don't scowl like that, Jen, it doesn't become you.'

'He's always been a loner,' Jenny grumbled. 'Ever since we've known him. How many women have I thrust under his nose in the last five years? And not one of them took. Not one!'

'He had affairs with a couple of them.'

'But nothing permanent,' she said crossly.

'Bryden's protracted bachelorhood is scarcely your concern, my love. Hurry up and change your dress and I'll take you to Michelle's.'

Michelle made desserts that normally could deflect Jenny from any of her concerns; it was a measure of her fondness for Bryden that she rubbed her nose on her husband's shirt-front and went on thoughtfully, 'His problem isn't really that dreadful accident that left him blind. Even though it must be *awful*. His problem goes a lot further back...I met his mother once, she would be enough to put you off women, certainly. But there must be more to it than that.'

'He's a self-sufficient, rational, cold-blooded scientist, who finds duality theorems more interesting than the curves of the opposite sex,' Matthew said. 'I'm sure you're the nearest he has to a female friend. Even so, Jenny, there's nothing you can do. So why don't——'

She was not listening. A brilliant smile suddenly lit up her face and her eyes glowed like emeralds. 'Matthew, I've just had a brainwave! Do your remember that charming young woman we met at Susan and Peter Drapers' last party? In April? What was her name? Casey! Casey Landrigan. I remember thinking Casey wasn't the right name for her at all—far too tomboyish. You must remember her, she was *very* beautiful.'

Matthew said cautiously, 'I believe I do remember her, now that you mention it. She was a distant cousin of Susan's, wasn't she?'

'That's right.' Jenny paused triumphantly. 'Guess what she does?'

With commendable patience Matthew said, 'I have no idea.'

'She trains guide-dogs. For the blind. How's that for coincidence?'

'You've just finished saying Bryden's main problem isn't his blindness. Anyway, I'm quite sure he doesn't want a dog.'

'She'll change his mind.'

'How can she? She doesn't know him—he wasn't at that party.'

'She will,' Jenny said confidently. 'Because I'm going to arrange it. You see, at the end of each class that she teaches, she gets a holiday. And she's teaching a class this month, she told me that, because she was worried about the effects of the heat on the dogs and the students.'

'Jenny, you cannot coerce an unknown young woman to spend her holidays with a complete stranger.'

'Not *with* him. Next door to him. Because who owns the cottage next to his?'

Matthew groaned. 'Susan and Peter Draper,' he supplied obediently. 'Seven years ago Peter mentioned that the cottage next door to theirs was for sale and we told Bryden because we knew he was looking for seashore property in Nova Scotia. So he bought it.'

'Exactly! I'll call Susan and tell her to offer the cottage to Casey in September. It's perfect!'

Matthew took a deep breath. Clasping his wife's shoulders, he said with the utmost seriousness, 'Jenny, you can't interfere in people's lives like that. It's immoral.'

A shadow of doubt crossed her face; Matthew did not often speak to her in that tone of voice. 'Truly?' she quavered.

'First of all, Bryden has to come to his own terms with his blindness—it's only been four months, after all. Secondly, if he has cut himself off from marriage, or even from long-term relationships, his reasons must be sufficient, powerful and private. And finally, a guide-dog trainer on holiday would not appreciate your throwing her at a man who happens to be blind.'

'But she was so *lovely*!'

'So were a good number of the other women you introduced Bryden to over the years. Drop it, Jenny.'

Jenny looked him in the eye and said without a trace of affection, 'I'm afraid for him, Matthew. Oh, not that he'll do anything foolish like swimming straight out to sea and not coming back, I don't mean that. But I'm afraid his...his courage will fail him. His inner strength. This self-sufficiency you talked about. I can't imagine anywhere more desolate than Ragged Island in February.'

Matthew had been to Ragged Island and agreed with her; its wild beauty could be lonely enough at the height of summer. Furthermore, over twelve years of marriage he had learned to trust in what he called Jenny's intuition. 'You could be right—he might turn into a real recluse.' He frowned. 'I still don't see what this Casey Landrigan can do.'

'In all honesty, neither do I. Because I agree with you, a dog isn't the issue at all. But she impressed me very strongly, and I don't just mean her looks.'

His frown deepened. 'There's nothing to lose by trying, I suppose,' he said reluctantly. 'Although she's probably got other plans for her vacation.'

'She's probably got a six-foot fiancé,' Jenny said gloomily.

'Cheer up, darling. At least you'll know you tried.'

'Bryden would be furious if he found out.'

'We won't tell him,' Matthew rejoined.

'Matthew Sibley, I love you.'

He kissed her very thoroughly. 'You just want me to treat you to raspberry cheesecake.'

'That, too,' Jenny said.

CHAPTER ONE

CASEY LANDRIGAN was standing at the bedroom window in the Drapers' cottage. The sun was shining, a fresh sea breeze was billowing the curtains against her body, and the gulls that drifted across the sky over the spruce trees and the granite cliffs were a dazzling white. An island offshore, rocky, spray-swept, took the brunt of tides and currents that had crossed the cold Atlantic unimpeded. Ragged Island. She had been here less than twenty-four hours and she was already in love with the place. Three weeks ago, she marvelled, she had not even known it existed. But for her cousin Susan, she still would not. But what better place to spend the precious eight days of her holiday?

She closed her eyes, savouring the cool, salt-laden wind. The last month in Ottawa had been unbearable. Hot, humid, the dogs listless, one of her students homesick, the other afflicted with hay fever. Even Douglas, the head trainer who was supervising the final months of her apprenticeship and who was normally the most even-tempered of men, had been short with her. She herself had come as close to doubting her vocation as she ever had.

She needed a holiday, she thought ruefully. She had caught sight of herself in a washroom mirror at the airport yesterday: shadows under her eyes, the skin pulled tight across her cheekbones, even her hair lustreless. Not all of it could be blamed on fluorescent lighting.

A gull flapped down to land on the crown of the spruce tree nearest the cottage; after an ungainly lurch or two, it settled its wings and presented Casey with a profile of hooked yellow beak and cold yellow eye. Its landing reminded her of the rather bumpy descent of the aircraft the day before; she was terrified of flying. But she had not wanted to waste four days of her vacation on the road.

What she did want was peace and quiet and no demands on her time. And this, she thought ecstatically, looked like the perfect place to find all three.

It certainly had privacy. Behind the cottage the driveway wound through fragrant pines to the main road and the village of Ragged Harbour, hidden in a dip in the land. The only other habitation in sight was the shingled roof of the next-door cottage, which Susan had vaguely intimated was occupied only in the summer.

Casey did not mind that it was empty. The last month had been inordinately full of people and their demands, and she had as usual given unstintingly of herself; to get away from the whole world for several days had seemed a wonderful idea. And a good way to start her vacation, she decided, was to spend the morning lying on the beach. Quickly she gathered up her gear, ran downstairs to the kitchen and ate some cereal and fruit, then dropped her book in her canvas tote bag. She would probably fall asleep before she read more than three or four pages. But that was all right—she was on holiday!

After pulling the door shut behind her, Casey stood on the veranda and took a deep breath of the clean, sweet air. The murmur of the waves soothed her ears. The sun fell warm on her bare arms and legs. Perfection, she thought. Sheer perfection. Could anyone be luckier than she?

She walked down the steps and across the grass, admiring the pansies and marigolds in the flower-beds. The gate squeaked as she pushed it open, and she stopped beside her rented car to get her bearings. Cut across the neighbour's property to go to the beach, Susan had told her; it was far quicker than skirting the cliffs that surrounded the cottage.

So Casey took the path on the other side of the driveway that led inland through the trees, whose needled boughs were swaying lazily in the breeze. The path soon doubled back towards the sea again, giving her tantalising glimpses of the curve of sand below. The beach would be sheltered, she thought smugly. Sheltered and private.

There was no noticeable boundary between the Drapers' property and that of their neighbour. Casey was rather pleased by this. There were far too many 'No Trespassing' signs in the world, she mused, her feet sinking in the carpet of fallen needles. Wars were fought over boundaries. Feuds erupted over the placing of fences. But who, in any real sense, could own the shimmering pattern of sunlight on the forest floor or the fragments of blue sky that pierced the swaying green boughs?

The woods suddenly ended, thrusting her on to a neatly mowed lawn. Stretched out on the lawn, face up, was a man.

Casey gave a strangled yelp that expressed surprise, shock and fear. The man's body, absolutely still, was clad in skimpy blue swimming-trunks; his eyes were hidden behind a type of sunglass that she particularly disliked, the kind that in two miniature mirrors reflected the face of the beholder. She could not even tell if he was awake or asleep. Or dead, she thought with a twinge of sheer terror, her eyes flicking round the empty clearing.

'I'm sorry!' she gasped idiotically. 'I didn't know anyone was here...are you all right?'

A shudder ran through the man's body as though he had woken too abruptly from a nightmare. Rubbing at his face with one hand, almost as if he had to reassure himself he was real, he reared up on one elbow, the glasses rendering his face blank of expression. 'Who are you?' he said harshly. 'What are you doing here?'

'I'm sorry I woke you,' Casey stumbled, although inwardly she was so grateful that he was alive that she did not sound as sorry as she might have. 'I didn't realise anyone was staying in this cottage.'

'I own it,' he answered, an unpleasant edge to his voice. 'Why shouldn't I be staying in it?'

'No reason whatsoever,' Casey said, wishing he did not sound so irritable. 'It's just that I was led to believe it would be empty.'

'By whom?'

Wishing he would take off his glasses so she could see his face, wondering if it could possibly match the muscled perfection of his body, Casey said politely, 'By the Drapers. Who were kind enough to lend me their cottage for the next few days.'

His breath hissed between his teeth; she did not need to see his face to sense an anger out of all proportion to anything she had said. 'Who *are* you?' he demanded.

She was beginning to grow angry herself; there was no need for him to be so unfriendly. Drawing herself to her full five feet nine, wishing her shorts and bikini top were not quite so brief, she answered with exaggerated courtesy, 'My name is Cassandra Elizabeth Landrigan, I am more commonly known as Casey, Susan Draper is my second cousin, I'm from Ontario and I'm here on holiday. Susan told me it was easier to get to the beach across your property...so that's what I was doing. I didn't mean to disturb you.' But I'm darned if I'm apologising again, she added inwardly.

He did not reciprocate by telling her his name. Instead he said grimly, 'I see. Well, I'm sorry to undo Susan's instructions, Miss Landrigan, but I would much prefer you not to use this path to the beach.' He gave her a curt nod. 'You might as well continue along it now that you're this far. But kindly go back along the cliffs.'

Her jaw dropped. Paradise had been invaded by the snake, and the perfection of the morning marred. 'It's a lot longer to go that way, isn't it?'

'I suppose so. However, you're on holiday, you said—you must have lots of time.'

She flushed. The 'No Trespassing' signs had been posted with a vengeance. 'I don't even know where the cliff path is,' she retorted.

'Go east from the beach around the headland. You'll see the steps up the cliff.' Another curt nod. 'Goodbye, Miss Landrigan.'

Casey tilted her chin. She said with a demureness that would have alerted someone like Douglas, 'Goodbye, Mr . . . but you haven't told me your name.'

Inexplicably his anger was very much in evidence again. 'You mean Susan didn't tell you?'

'I would scarcely be asking you if she had.'

'There's no need for you to know my name—we won't be meeting again. . .I'm sorry if I sound rude, but I guard my privacy very jealously.' As if to signal that the conversation was over, he turned on his stomach.

The muscles rippled along his spine. His skin, taut across his ribs, was tanned a light gold; a great deal of it seemed to be exposed. Dragging her eyes away, Casey said stiffly, 'I came here to get away from everyone, too. So I most certainly will not be bothering a neighbour as unwelcoming as you. . .and I don't think you're the least bit sorry that you sounded rude.'

Knowing her last remark had been childish in the extreme, she stalked past the man's recumbent form. Behind him the lawn sloped up to his cottage. Although to call it a cottage was a form of reverse snobbery, Casey thought crossly, taking a moment to study it. An architect must have designed its subtle blending of cedar, stone and glass that made it an integral part of the evergreens that shaded its slanting roof. Wisely the garden had been left in its natural state, with a brook meandering through the maples on the far side of the clearing, its soft plashing in counterpoint to the sigh of the wind. The beauty of the place caught at her throat, making her even angrier.

She found the break in the trees that marked the path to the beach and headed across the grass towards it. When she reached it, she risked a backward look. The man was still lying on his stomach, his head buried in his arms. Asleep already, she thought. She'd meant no more to him than a fly he would brush from his shoulder.

As she was enveloped by the trees again, she found herself wondering what colour his eyes were. His hair was a darker brown than her own, unruly hair rather in need of cutting. Perhaps it would compromise his privacy to go to the barber's, she thought nastily. With that colour hair his eyes could be any colour: blue or grey or brown. Grey would be her bet. Grey like stone. Or storm-clouds. Or steel.

Casey suddenly realised she was tramping through the woods as though she were on her way to a fire. She was even breathing hard. Trying to be amused by this, but not really succeeding, she consciously focused on the rhythm of the surf and the glimpses of sand that filtered through the trees, and slowed her steps. She did not want her first view of the beach to be spoiled by a temper tantrum.

A minute or two later she came to wooden stairs, cedar-stained, that led down to the sand. The beach was V-shaped, sheltered from the wind by the cliffs and the trees, and again something in her responded instantly to the seclusion and beauty of the scene. She was the only person in sight. Had it not been for that unpleasant incident with her neighbour, she would have been perfectly happy.

She spread her towel on the sand, anointed herself with sun-screen, and determinedly began to read. But the man's face, shuttered behind the glasses, kept intruding itself between her and the page, until finally she gave up and stared out to sea, where the island guarded the shore and broke the force of the waves. Why had he affected her so strongly?

She found that she could recall every detail of the man's body, the dark hair that curled on his chest and legs, the narrow hips, the smooth play of muscle in his shoulders. Even his voice, resonant with authority, rang in her ears. Yet she did not know his name, and if he had his way they would never see each other again. For her to feel disappointment as acute as any she had ever known was ridiculous.

She was not used to men being rude to her. Her father was a man very much in touch with his feelings, capable of expressing his rare anger in a constructive way, and while her three brothers had been guilty of the normal horseplay in a growing family there had never been real animosity behind it. She had had her fair share of dates, tending to pick young men who most reminded her of her father. Douglas reminded her of her father. Douglas, she was almost sure, would be seriously in pursuit of her once her apprenticeship was finished and he no longer had a supervisory role over her. She was in no hurry. But she liked him very much.

This man was not like her father. Or Douglas. So why was she allowing him to ruin the first day of her holiday? After all, she had come here for privacy. She could scarcely deny him his.

Eventually Casey got up from her towel and wandered down to the edge of the sea, then picked her way among the tide pools in the rocks, until slowly sun and surf worked their spell and she regained most of the carefree happiness of early morning. Not even the discovery later in the day that the cliff path was both long and arduous could destroy her peace of mind. This was her holiday. She was going to enjoy it.

Casey went jogging later in the afternoon, discovering a network of dirt roads near the cottage; she slept peacefully for nearly ten hours, and woke to the patter of rain on the roof. So she spent most of the next day in the cottage, reading, baking biscuits, and listening to records in front of the fire.

The following day, her third at Ragged Island, dawned clear and bright. There was no wind; the sea gleamed like a mirror. Like her neighbour's glasses, thought Casey as she stood at the bedroom window, and found that the memory still had the power to hurt. She would go to the beach after breakfast, but she would go by the cliff path. She would not risk another confrontation.

The news on the radio warned of an approaching low-pressure system with high winds and heavy rain; incredible though this seemed on so peaceful a morning, Casey must have believed it, because she found herself hurrying through her breakfast to spend as much time as possible on the beach. So it was early when she rounded the headland and saw the curve of pale sand in front of her.

But not early enough. Her misanthropic neighbour was there before her.

Casey stopped in dismay. He was sitting hunched on the sand, staring out to sea, his body angled away from her. He had not seen her, nor could he have heard her approach; she could turn tail and he would be none the wiser.

For a moment she was tempted to do so. The beach was small—too small for the two of them. She could lie on the grass in front of the cottage instead.

But then something in his pose struck her: a rigidity, an absolute stillness that was almost frightening. What was he thinking about, this tall stranger with his lean, beautiful body and his obsessive need to be alone? Why was he so tangibly unhappy?

And, more to the point, why should she allow him to drive her off a strip of sand that below the high-tide line was public property?

Gripping her tote bag a little more tightly than was necessary, Casey marched across the beach. A seagull screamed overhead and a flock of sandpipers skittered away from her on legs like tiny twigs. About fifty feet from the hunched figure on the sand, she put down her bag and spread out her towel. He was still gazing at the horizon.

She stripped to her bikini and sat down. He paid her no attention. She took out her book, a fat historical romance whose heroine, spirited, dashing and seductive, would have made mincemeat out of the stranger. He ignored her. She made rather a production of rubbing on her sun-screen. No reaction.

Casey discovered that her serenity had vanished, to be replaced by the slow boil of rage. The glitter of sun on the waves seemed to mock her, while the cries of the gulls were derisive. Privacy was all very well, she fumed, but it would not hurt him to at least say hello.

She forced her attention back to her book. Her heroine in less than two pages managed to free herself from the bonds around her wrists, confront her captor—who bore a strong resemblance to the stranger on the beach—and shoot him with a pistol, then steal a horse to make good her escape. Casey stood up. Enough was enough.

The sand was hot on the soles of her feet. When she was within twenty feet of the man, she called out in a carrying voice, 'Good morning! Isn't it a lovely day?'

He gave an overdone start, his head swinging in her direction. He was wearing the same dark glasses. She added kindly, 'You're getting a touch of sunburn on your shoulders; you really should use sun-screen.'

He said slowly, 'Miss Cassandra Elizabeth Landrigan.'

'So you remember my name—I'm flattered.'

'Don't be. I rarely forget facts.'

'How useful,' Casey said smoothly. 'I wish I were more like that. But if you were to tell me your name, I promise I'd do my best to remember it.'

He replied just as smoothly, 'It would be unkind of me to tax your mental capacity.'

She could feel her temper rising again. Determined to be pleasant, she said, 'Are you going for a swim?'

'No.'

'I'm a bit nervous of swimming alone, even though Susan said it was quite safe here—no undertow. Do you mind keeping an eye on me?'

'I'm about to leave,' he said brusquely.

Casey took a deep breath. 'You really don't want anything to do with me, do you?'

'I thought I'd made that clear the other day.'

'I was giving you the benefit of the doubt...we all have days when we get out of bed the wrong side.' She added, 'I do wish you'd take those glasses off—I feel as though I'm talking to a plate-glass window.'

'Whereas,' he said with dangerous quietness, 'I feel as though I'm talking to a thick-skinned young woman who's incapable of taking a hint.'

Casey flinched, aware of the salt sting of tears. She said furiously, 'Very well! Since I have as much right to be on this beach as you, I suggest you stick to this half and I'll stick to the other, and I promise I shall not repeat my mistake of acting like a reasonably polite human being—it's obviously wasted on you!'

She whirled and ran back to her towel. She had had the last word, but it was a hollow victory. Grabbing her book, she tried to read, but the words swam together on the page and the heroine's feisty manner, rather than behaviour to be emulated, now seemed merely silly. Real life was not like that. Real life was the most attractive man she'd ever met in her life being quite abominably rude to her for no reason that made any sense.

She sneaked a sideways glance through her lashes. He was still sitting there, still contemplating the horizon. So his excuse that he was leaving and therefore could not watch her swim had been a lie; he simply didn't want to be bothered.

It would serve him right if she drowned under his nose, she thought darkly. However, she did not think she would attempt this as a tactic to gain his attention. He would be quite capable of letting her sink to the bottom of the sea.

She then discovered she was blinking back tears again. What was wrong with her? At the school she was frequently commended for her disposition: kind, calm, unruffled Casey, who could be counted on to keep her head in any situation. Who never let the students get to her. Who had infinite patience with the dogs. Yet this one man, whose name she did not even know, had the

capacity to arouse her to anger, disappointment and—
she lowered her eyes to her book—desire.

She had wanted to sit down beside him on the beach;
she had wanted to touch him; she had wanted to smooth
the tension from his shoulders with her palms and run
her fingers through his hair.

Her movements jerky and hurried, Casey shoved her
book back in her bag, picked up her towel and got to
her feet. Turning her back on the seated man, she walked
with as much dignity as she could muster towards the
headland, where the incoming tide swirled around the
rocks. Picking her way among them, wincing at the initial
chill of the water, she was soon beneath the channelled
grey cliffs, the complaints of the gulls loud in her ears.
She was also out of sight of the man on the beach, and
was aware of an almost palpable relief. She kept going,
clambering over the larger boulders, walking on the sand
whenever possible, and finally climbing the steep flight
of steps that belonged to the Drapers. Although she was
out of breath at the top, she did not stop until she came
to the lawn in front of the cottage. The sun was warmer
here than on the beach. Spreading out her towel, Casey
lay down on the grass.

She must not talk to the man again. No more hellos
on the beach, no more requests that he watch her swim.
She would treat him just as if he were a chunk of granite
on the sand, a part of the scenery to be ignored, of no
more interest than a gull or a passing ship. She would
not allow him to spoil her holiday; she had worked too
hard for it and needed it too much. He meant nothing
to her. Nothing.

For the first time since she had arrived at Ragged
Island, Casey wished she had company. Specifically,
Douglas's company; he would make her forget the
stranger on the beach. But Douglas took his pro-

fessional ethics very seriously, and would not contemplate spending a vacation with her while she was still his apprentice.

Casey heaved a sigh, feeling definitely out of sympathy with professional ethics, and went in the cottage to get some fruit juice. Life, at times, was hard to fathom.

By afternoon the horizon wore a ruff of purple-edged clouds and the wind had freshened; dusk came early, for the clouds now hung low over the sky and gusts of rain drove against the window-panes. Casey was glad to be indoors. She drew the curtains, lit a fire in the stone hearth, and took out the pullover she was knitting for her niece Leeanne, daughter of her elder sister Anne. She liked to knit. But she went to bed early, for it was a day she somehow wanted to put behind her. Tomorrow would be better, she thought sleepily. Tomorrow she would explore the village; and she would stay away from the beach.

However, four hours later Casey was wide awake. The news broadcaster had been all too accurate in his forecast, for the wind was howling around the cottage, rattling the windows and carrying with it the deeper roar of the sea. She tried burying her head under the pillow to dull the noise, not sure whether she should be afraid or exhilarated. One thing was certain: she could not go back to sleep. Eventually she got out of bed and went to the window.

In the eerie glow cast by the moon, which appeared and reappeared between the ragged-edged clouds, the branches of the pines were tossing in the wind like frail ships adrift in a riptide; the island offshore had vanished behind sheets of driven foam.

Another adjective frequently used to describe Casey at the school was 'sensible'. She discovered the storm did not make her feel in the least sensible. She wanted to be out in it, a part of it; she wanted to stand near the edge of the cliffs and fill her ears with the rage of the surf and feel the salt spray trickle down her cheeks.

Why not? It was no longer raining. And she was certainly not likely to meet anyone else at this hour of the night.

Before she could change her mind—one part of which was sure Douglas would not approve of her crashing through the woods in the middle of the night at the height of a storm—she got dressed in jeans, a sweater and a wind-cheater, and went downstairs. The wind almost ripped the front door from her hand; she slammed it shut and headed for the cliff path.

Douglas, she thought as she struggled down the path, could have been right. The trees creaked and groaned, the gale keened, the ocean's roar grew louder. Bent forward, she scurried through the woods, her eyes adjusting to the half-light of the moon. She'd look silly if she tripped over a root and fell. Sillier still if a branch crashed on her head.

But the scene that met Casey's gaze at the end of the path was worth every step of the way. At the foot of the cliffs among the churn of foam and the rearing waves the blunt-nosed boulders stood firm, like primitive sea-lions; the noise was deafening. She took shelter under a tree, searching out the tiny strip of beach, now piled high with seaweed and driftwood. Beyond it was the property of her neighbour. Although the cliffs were less sheer over there, they seemed more exposed to the ocean's fury. Even as she watched, a great cloud of spray exploded into the air with a loud thump that overrode the cacophony of the storm.

A blowhole, she thought, her eyes gleaming. Thirty seconds later the water erupted again with a thud like distant dynamite.

Anyone as disagreeable as her neighbour would not be out on a night like this, Casey was sure. He'd be asleep in bed. She was going to trespass on his property and get a closer look.

She hurried back up to her cottage, then took the trail to the beach. She could remember a fork in the trail before it came to the steps that led down to the sand; she'd be willing to bet that that fork led to the blowhole.

The house next door—she refused to call it a cottage— was in total darkness. She pulled a face at the upstairs windows and fought her way across the grass. When she re-entered the forest, the trees offered almost no shelter from the wind. A branch slapped her face. A pine-cone whisked past her cheek.

She had to wait a minute for the moon to reappear before she could locate the trail that led away from the beach to the cliffs. The undergrowth was thicker here and the trees crowded more closely together, the trunks black as pitch against the moonlit sky, the boughs flapping like the wings of crows. Twigs, finger-like, plucked at her sleeves. Aware of a sudden unease as strong as it was irrational, Casey battled onward.

Whump! went the blowhole, and the driven spray wet her cheeks and made her blink. Into the sudden lull, like a gunshot, a branch cracked in two.

She froze, her heart pounding, but the moon chose that moment to disappear behind a cloud, so she could see nothing through the tangled black branches. That's because there's nothing there to see, she told herself firmly. Don't let your imagination get the better of you.

The clouds parted. In the pale, ghostly light she distinctly saw movement, a huddled black shape near the edge of the cliff. Then the wind lashed the boughs of the spruce trees and the shape vanished among all the other shapes.

A figment of your imagination, Casey. There's nothing there.

But she found she was rooted to the spot, the blowhole no longer the lure it had been. She was crazy to be out in the woods in a gale. Out of her mind. Under the ceaseless roar of the ocean anything could creep up on her and she would never hear it. Never even see it. She should be home in her bed.

But as she turned to leave her eyes flickered nervously towards the cliff and she saw it again: the dark bulk of a body blundering among the trees. Terrified, she dug her nails into the trunk of the nearest tree. What was it? A bear? But there weren't any bears in Nova Scotia . . . were there?

Casey was not sure she wanted an answer to that question. Her imagination, fed by the wildness of the night and the fitful pallor of the moon, took another leap forward. It was a deer. A deer that had injured itself on the rocks.

She'd better go and see, she couldn't just leave it there to suffer. Nor would she be able to sleep for the rest of the night if she didn't satisfy her curiosity. Carefully noting the position of the path so she could find it again, she gathered all her courage and began threading her way through the trees, ducking to avoid low-hanging branches, every sense alert.

Her imagination had not created the figure among the rocks. It was real. It also seemed to be moving closer to the edge of the cliff. Then it suddenly straightened, and with a pang of sheer terror Casey realised it was a human being, its arms flailing the air. It staggered into the angled trunk of a fallen poplar and rebounded against the rocks. Rocks that made an unstable wall between the forest floor and the sheer drop to the sea below.

She yelled as loudly as she could, 'Don't move—stay still!' The wind tore the words from her lips and the night swallowed them. She began to run.

CHAPTER TWO

BOUGHS, wet from rain and spray, dashed water in Casey's face as she dodged between the trees. Her jacket caught on a snag; she yanked at the sleeve, not caring that it tore. Stumbling over the rough ground, she shouted again, 'Stay where you are!' She could see now that the figure was that of a man, crouched among the rocks.

Casey cleared the fallen poplar trunk in a leap she would never have attempted in daylight, got her balance and thrust herself between the man and the edge of the cliff. 'Are you trying to *kill* yourself?' she gasped. 'You're only ten feet from the edge!'

Then the ground shuddered. A curtain of spray burst from the blowhole and, whipped by the wind, drenched them both in cold salt water. Casey grabbed at his arm and heard herself scream, 'I don't even know your name!'

For the man was her neighbour. His face was ghastly in the pale grey light, the eye sockets like black pits, his hair streaking his forehead. He had cut himself, so that mingled blood and water trickled down his cheek. He also seemed to have lost his voice.

Casey shook his arm; he was wearing a dark shirt that clung damply to his skin. 'What in God's name are you doing here?' she demanded, she who never swore. 'You frightened the life out of me! I thought you were going over the edge.'

He muttered something in a low, choked voice. Her body stilled as a cold fist seemed to clutch her heart.

She did not know what he had said, and was afraid to ask him to repeat it. She did know she had to get him away from here, up to the house, to warmth and light and the shelter of four walls. His face was only inches from hers, the deep-set eyes staring fixedly over her head. She said with a compassion so fierce that it shook her to the roots of her being, 'Come on—let's go up to the house.'

Awkwardly, because she was still clutching his sleeve, he stood upright; he was four or five inches taller than she. His body was shaking as if he had a fever. 'I don't know the way,' he said in a low voice.

For a horrified moment she wondered if she was alone in the woods with a madman. 'But you live here,' she faltered. 'We're not that far from the house.'

The muscles clenched under her fingers. He said harshly, 'I'm blind...hadn't you guessed?'

For a moment Casey was paralysed with shock. Then, swift as lightning, all the tiny indications that she, of all people, should not have missed dropped into place. The dark glasses. His start when she had spoken to him on the beach. His refusal to watch her swim. Even his obsessive need for privacy. But before she could say anything the dull thud of trapped water again reverberated under her feet. 'Duck!' she said urgently, and pulled his head down into the shelter of her shoulder.

The spray, driven by the gale, stung her cheek and dribbled down her neck. She released him, remembering with startling clarity the hard line of bone under his wet hair, and said with a calmness that was quite false, 'No, I hadn't guessed. Come on, we'll go up to the house together.'

But he did not move. 'Susan didn't tell you?'

'All Susan said was that the cottage next door was only used in summer—she was far too busy telling me about bedding and the switches for the power and water, and what to do if squirrels had got into the pantry.' A frown creased Casey's forehead. 'If you're blind, where's your cane? Don't tell me you came down here without it.'

'I lost it back there in the woods,' he said so tonelessly that she had to strain to hear him. Then the words came pouring out. 'I've always loved storms, even as a kid. Ever since I bought this place I've been fascinated by the blowhole—the locals call it the Devil's Ear, and the tides and the wind have to be just right for it to work. Tonight I figured I could find my way down here without any trouble, I've been here a hundred times, and even if I couldn't see the spray I could hear it and get some sense of the ocean and the storm.' His body was racked by a spasm that had nothing to do with the cold. 'I can't even manage that! After I dropped my cane I panicked . . . lost my bearings, couldn't find the path, didn't know where the cliff was . . . lost in the woods like a four-year-old.'

His voice was caustic with self-disgust. It would have been all too easy for Casey to have given him sympathy; her heart ached for him. Instead she said what a few moments ago she had been afraid to say. 'So you didn't come down here to throw yourself over the cliff?'

'God, no! I don't think I ever contemplated that, not even right after the accident.' His face set in grim lines, he muttered, 'I must have looked like a fool, floundering around in all those rocks . . . a goddamned fool.'

She could imagine all too well his humiliation. A grown man lost in the woods and rescued by a woman to whom he had been exceedingly rude was not an enviable role. She said crisply, 'You'd have been fine if you hadn't lost your cane. And it's little wonder you lost your bearings——'

Once again the thunder of confined water shook the earth beneath their feet. But this time it was he who abruptly turned her about and pressed her face to his chest to protect her from the spray, taking its lash on his back.

Casey stood very still. He was holding her impersonally, she was sure, his motives nothing more than belated good manners; no reason for her to feel as though heaven had opened its doors and beckoned her in. Certainly no reason to feel she could spend the rest of the night in his arms among the wind-tossed trees.

He pushed her away and said roughly, 'Let's get the hell out of here.'

With an actual physical effort Casey made herself sound natural and relaxed. 'Take my elbow,' she said, 'and I'll lead the way. We'll have to keep our heads down until we find the path.'

She set off up the slope, warning him of rocks, holding up boughs that might have struck him in the face, and all the time she was acutely aware of the strong grip of his fingers at her elbow. He resented having to trail behind her, she would swear, and asked without any of her usual tact, 'How long have you been blind?'

'Five months.'

His clipped voice discouraged further questions. Casey said with transparent relief, 'Here's the path again—but I can't see your cane. If we don't find it tonight, I'll look for it in the morning.'

'No need—I've got another one in the house.'

He could not have said more clearly that he did not want her wandering around his property in the morning: did not want to be further indebted to her. Furious with him for rebuffing her, furious with herself for caring, Casey marched up the path, her arm rigid in his clasp. 'You might at least introduce yourself,' she said frostily.

'If you'd slow down a bit I would.'

She stopped dead, so that he almost cannoned into her. 'So now your lack of courtesy is *my* fault?'

The moonlight filtering through the trees showed her that he was smiling; a smile that looked as if it had not been exercised very much lately, but was nevertheless a smile. 'You have a temper, Cassandra Elizabeth Landrigan,' he said.

'Casey,' she spat. 'Casey will do just fine.'

He raised one brow. 'And I'd guess you're about sixteen?'

Even over the shrill of the wind he must have heard her indrawn breath. 'You have to be the most insulting man I have ever met!'

He brought his free hand up and unerringly traced the line of her jaw. 'You're not a day over thirty. No sag.'

'I am twenty-three years old, and I will have you know that women do not sag, as you so delicately put it, until they're in their fifties. So I could be considerably older than thirty!'

'You're forgetting I had my arms around you back there by the cliff,' he said with an intonation that made her blush fierily in the darkness. 'Anyway, I knew from your voice the first time I heard you speak that you were young.'

'But not as young as sixteen!' Consciously unclenching her fists, she added coldly, 'Now it's my turn—your name, please. And you might as well tell me your age, too. Just to keep things equal.'

Any remnants of his smile vanished. 'Equal?' he snarled. 'That's a laugh.'

Deliberately misunderstanding him, she said, 'It is rather—I've never met anyone as overpowering as you.'

With cruel strength his fingers tightened their hold. 'So you don't think blindness is a barrier to any kind of a normal relationship?' he demanded.

'No, I don't.'

He dropped her arm with a smothered curse. 'Then you don't know anything about it.'

He had given her the perfect opportunity to say that she knew a great deal about it. But something kept her silent. 'Your name?' she repeated gently.

'Bryden. Bryden Moore. With two ''o''s and an ''e''. Aged twenty-nine.'

Casey said, mischief warming her voice, 'Now that we've been formally introduced we could continue this conversation in the house—I'm soaking wet.'

He said stiffly, 'I'd appreciate it if you'd take me as far as the house.'

The moon was behind a cloud, so his face was in shadow. But the message was clear: he still wanted nothing to do with her. We'll see about that, thought Casey, and held out her elbow. 'Let's go,' she said.

The rest of the journey was accomplished in silence, with the wind at their backs and the sound of the surf gradually diminishing. She led him round a rock wall to the side of the house, said evenly, 'The door's straight ahead of you,' and waited.

He said with a formal inclination of his head, 'Thank you for your help. I won't ask you in—it's late.'

'You'll have to do better than that,' Casey said clearly. 'The fact that it's three in the morning has nothing to do with why you're not asking me in—at least pay me the compliment of telling the truth.'

His lips thinned. 'I'm tired and cold and I don't feel like company—is that better?'

'*My* company,' she said with real hurt. 'You've made that clear from the beginning.'

'Anyone's company!'

'So who are you hiding from?' she flashed. 'The whole world? Because you're blind?'

'I can't stand people feeling sorry for me!'

'At the moment I'm so angry with you that the only person I feel sorry for is myself for having you as a neighbour,' Casey cried incoherently. 'We're *neighbours*! I'm only here another five days; it wouldn't hurt you to ask me in and make hot chocolate and I could wash that cut over your eye and put on a band-aid. It would be a friendly thing to do and I wouldn't want to do it any more or any less if you had your sight, that's got nothing to do with it.'

There could be no mistaking her sincerity. The lines of Bryden's mouth relaxed and for a moment she thought she had won. He said, a note in his voice she had not heard before, 'That's nice of you, Casey Landrigan... but I'm still not going to ask you in. My reasons are personal and private and I know you don't——'

'There's someone with you—a woman!' Casey gasped, her whole body suddenly bathed in cold sweat. 'I never thought of that! I'm sorry, I didn't mean to intrude.' She should have realised he would not be alone; every woman in the countryside must be after him.

Clipping off his words, Bryden said, 'There's no one with me, woman or otherwise. It's very simple, Casey— we have nothing to say to each other. As you mentioned, you're only here a few more days. You go your way and I'll go mine... it's better that way.'

He might just as well have slammed the door in her face. Wanting to burst into loud and undignified tears, knowing she would die rather than do so, Casey said flatly, 'I get the message—finally. I'm sorry I was such a slow learner, but where I grew up we treat the word neighbour very differently. I promise I won't bother you again, Mr Moore. Goodbye.'

It was one of the hardest things she had ever done in her life to turn on her heel and walk away from him; but she did it. She had no choice. Nor did he call her back, or even say goodbye. When she reached the edge of the woods, where the path led to her cottage, she looked back over her shoulder. Bryden had gone inside and the door was closed, its blank brown face mocking her.

The next day Casey did not go near the beach; she could not have swum anyway, for the sea was generously spattered with whitecaps. Instead she drove into the village, where she bought some groceries, had lunch at a café and poked around in the antique shops. Then, after a five-mile jog along the back roads, she cooked fish for supper and read in front of the fireplace. The other thing she did was try very hard not to think about her neighbour.

She did not altogether succeed. She carried with her all day a steady ache in the vicinity of her heart, a nagging pain that neither reason nor activity could dispel. Casey was not used to being rebuffed by members of the opposite sex. Without vanity, she knew she was an attractive woman who enjoyed the company of men; men, in consequence, seemed to enjoy her company. This was not true, however, of Bryden Moore: he had evinced a positive distaste for her company.

But there was more to it than that. She liked Douglas very much, and for some time had sensed that he more than liked her; she was perfectly content to wait the last eight months of her apprenticeship to see if indeed he did. No impatience. No hurry. Whereas Bryden, with whom she had had three brief and highly unsatisfactory encounters, aroused in her a fury of impatience and frustration. She had only a few days of her holidays left. She wanted to march over to his house and throw herself at the door and pound on it until he had no choice but to let her in.

And then what? Be ordered off the premises, like a love-struck teenager?

Why, Casey? she asked herself, abandoning the book to gaze into the dying fire. Why are you even contemplating a course of action so foreign to your nature?

As if Aunt Bridget, her mother's elder sister, were in the room, she could hear the echo of her voice. Casey's such a nice girl. So thoughtful. So kind... Bryden did not make her feel nice, or thoughtful, or kind. Bryden brought out another Casey, a young woman who was wild and hungry and restless as the sea; a Casey she herself had never known existed.

This new Casey frightened her. Another dimension to her personality had been revealed by an inadvertent meeting with a stranger. A man who happened to be, by a supreme irony of fate, blind.

The last little flame collapsed upon itself into an orange glow of heat; sparks like miniature fireworks were eclipsed by the blackness of the chimney. With a heavy sigh Casey got to her feet and went to bed.

The following morning the sea was as smooth as glass, reflecting the cloudless blue of the sky. The trees were still, and the strip of sand a dazzling white in the sun. Going into the other bedroom, the one that overlooked Bryden's house, Casey subjected his property to a close scrutiny. She was sure she could see someone moving around in the front garden. If Bryden was in the garden he was not at the beach. So she would go to the beach.

Carrying her portable radio, which dispelled a lone-liness she was not ready to admit to, Casey headed for the wooden steps at the far boundary of the Drapers' property. She had no trouble rounding the headland today due to the low tide; because she knew she was alone, she was singing quite loudly, assisting John Denver and Placido Domingo with a soprano more noteworthy for enthusiasm than pitch. Then, in mid-phrase, she broke off.

Bryden *was* on the beach. He had heard her coming—who would not have? she thought in a mixture of morti-fication and panic—and had got to his feet, facing her. He began crossing the beach towards her. 'Casey?' he said.

Her feet felt as heavy as rocks in the warm sand. 'No! Yes!' she gasped. 'I'm leaving—right away. I only came down here because I saw someone around your house so I thought I'd have the beach to myself. Bryden, go away! You're *ruining* my vacation.' In a cracked voice she heard herself add, 'And why is it that whenever you come within twenty feet of me I *sound* like a sixteen-year-old?'

He was much nearer than twenty feet now, walking at a steady pace straight towards her. Ten feet. Five feet. Two feet. Then he stopped. He was wearing the glasses she hated so much, and this gave her the courage to say with asperity, 'There's nothing wrong with your hearing, that's for sure.'

'John Denver will never know what he's missed.'

'I was not referring to my singing,' she said haughtily.

'Ah...if you mean how I can walk across a beach to within touching distance of you,' he reached out one hand and brushed the bare skin of her arm, 'that's not just the sound of your voice. I can smell your perfume, too.'

Struck dumb, her eyes darkening with involuntary emotion, Casey gazed up at him, and saw in his glasses her own twin image, wisps of hair about her face, her lips unsmiling. He went on calmly, 'You probably saw Simon in the garden. Simon McIver. He used to be the lightkeeper on Ragged Island until they put in an automatic light. Now he does a little fishing and looks after the grounds of some of the summer places. In fact, I think he looks after Susan's in the spring and the fall.'

'Oh. I think Susan did mention his name.'

Bryden had approached her this time, not the reverse; and in comparison to their other meetings he looked positively friendly. Somehow this gave Casey courage. Searching for the right words, she went on quietly, 'Bryden, I hate talking to you when you're hiding behind those glasses. I don't know what kind of an accident cost you your sight...but even if your eyes are—are deformed in some way, I'd rather see them as they really are. Please?'

She had no idea how he would react. She waited, her heart hammering so loudly that she was afraid he would hear it, and saw him reach up and take off his glasses.

His eyes were blue, an indigo-blue, smoky, full of mysterious depths; around them was a network of tiny white scars, and over one brow the cut, already healing, from the night of the storm. Had his eyes not been focused an inch or two below the level of her own, she would never have known he was blind. Her throat tight, she stepped closer to him, took his hand and brought it to her forehead. 'I'm taller than the average female,' she said huskily.

He said in a low voice, 'I wish to God I could see you.'

He was stroking the hair back from her forehead, although she was not sure that he was aware of what he was doing. Because it did not seem to her to be a time for false modesty, she said, 'I've been told I'm beautiful. Certainly you're the first man who's ever given me the brush-off quite so consistently.'

His hand slid down her cheek and the slender line of her neck to her shoulder. 'I was convinced I was doing the right thing,' he said, his face so bleak that she had to fight against the impulse to put her arms around him.

Instead she asked the obvious question. 'So why did you speak to me today?'

His hand fell to his side. 'I don't know—I couldn't help myself. You sounded so happy, singing away as you came round the rocks... Did you mean what you said the other night, about it making no difference that I'm blind?'

'Yes. I meant it.'

'Blindness is a terrible handicap!'

'Yes, it is,' she said steadily. 'But you—the essential you, the person who is Bryden—you're the same.'

'I've always been a loner.' Then he gave his head a little shake. 'There's something about you—I always end up saying far more than I intended.'

Intuitively she knew better than to pursue this. She said pertly, 'So if I suggest we go for a swim, will you bite my head off?'

She had taken him by surprise. 'Swim? Now?'

'Why not? It's a perfect day.'

There was naked longing in his face. 'I haven't been swimming since last summer.'

'I'm sure you haven't forgotten how,' Casey teased. 'By the look of those biceps, you're probably Olympic class.'

This time he did smile, a smile that literally took her breath away. 'Flattery, Cassandra?'

'Whatever works,' she answered airily.

'Can I leave my shirt and glasses with your stuff?'

'Sure.'

As Bryden hauled his T-shirt over his head, Casey took a step backwards in sheer self-defence. She had grown up with three brothers and had been to the beach with several young men over the years, but nothing had prepared her for the surge of primitive desire that seized her at the closeness of Bryden's body. She had never felt like this in her life, she thought frantically, and the self-image she had always taken for granted of placid, level-headed Casey took a step backwards as well.

'What's the matter?' Bryden said sharply.

'Nothing!' she sputtered, adding with complete illogicality, 'How do you know something's the matter?'

'I . . . just seem able to sense whatever you're feeling,' he said slowly.

With admirable insouciance Casey replied, 'You're what my younger sister Kathy, who's the baby of the family, would call a hunk. It's nothing a dip in the cold Atlantic won't fix—come along.'

But he resisted the tug of her hand. 'What colour's your hair, Casey?'

'Brown.'

'Your eyes?'

'Blue. Although not nearly such a beautiful blue as yours.'

He grimaced. 'It's so damned frustrating . . . if only I could see you, just for a split second.'

'We're going for a swim, Bryden.'

His sudden grin was vibrant with life. 'You have the temper of a wildcat and you're used to getting your own way with the opposite sex. Correct me if I'm wrong.'

'Whereas you're stubborn and strong-willed. No corrections permitted.'

'You got it.'

They were standing a couple of feet apart, their hands loosely linked. Casey said matter-of-factly, as she began leading him towards the water's edge, 'The rocks are well to your left, so if you head straight out you can't come to any harm. I'll stay nearer to shore—I'll yell if you should get way off course.'

The sand was damp now underfoot, and then the first chill ripples broke over her toes. She gave an exaggerated shiver. 'This was my idea, wasn't it? I must have been crazy.'

But Bryden was not listening. The profile he had turned to her, as strongly carved as the cliffs behind him, was immobile; had she not known better, she would have sworn he was staring at the horizon. He gave her fingers a quick squeeze. 'Thanks, Casey,' he muttered. Then he let go and ran headlong into the water. When he was waist-deep he plunged under the surface, emerging in the trough between two breakers, his hair slicked to his skull. In a strong overarm crawl he started swimming out to sea.

He swam with a fierce energy, like an animal that had been cooped up too long in a cage. Every now and then he dived under the waves as though they were his natural element, the place where he was at home, then burst into the air again as playfully as a porpoise.

Slowly Casey waded out into the water. There was a lump in her throat, for she was seeing a Bryden she had not seen before: this was the real man, a man of power and vigour exulting in his freedom; a man as different from the crouched and defeated figure among the rocks as day was from night. Afraid of the intensity of her emotions, she began to swim, letting the waves buffet her body, her eyes never leaving the swimmer churning tirelessly through the water.

Bryden swam for a long time. Then he lay on his back, floating aimlessly, and although Casey would not have disturbed him for the world, she could not help wondering what he was thinking about, with his face turned to the sky and the waves rocking his body. Eventually he let the incoming tide carry him towards the shore; he was doing a lazy breast-stroke, as though reluctant to give up the buoyancy of the ocean for the ungiving solidity of land.

She called out to him as he drew closer, and he changed course, reaching her in half a dozen long strokes. Lightly she touched his wet shoulder. 'Did you have a good swim?'

He stood up, shaking the spray from his hair like a puppy, the darker hair on his chest sleek as a pelt. Encircling her waist with his hands, he lifted her high over his head and held her there, his face alive with laughter, his white teeth gleaming. 'Wonderful!' he exclaimed.

Casey gave a breathless laugh. 'I'm heavy—put me down!'

'I could lift ten of you,' he boasted.

With a delightful chuckle she responded, 'But how fortunate you don't have to prove it.'

'Are you calling my bluff?'

'I do believe I am,' she said demurely.

Abruptly he lowered her into the water, and as he did so a breaker, white-crested, thrust her against his chest. He tightened his grip automatically. Casey stood very still, her face raised to his, feeling as though time itself had stopped, leaving her in a place where she had always, without knowing it, wanted to be.

'Casey?' Bryden said. 'Casey...'

As he lowered his head, she met him halfway, her lips unashamedly hungry, her body trembling lightly in his embrace. He kissed her as though it were years since he had held and kissed a woman, as though only she existed to him in the whole wide world. She responded with reckless generosity, and in so doing crossed into a territory where she had never been before.

The tide was flowing more strongly now, and the wave that struck Casey's back made her stagger in Bryden's arms. He shifted his weight to keep his own balance, and somehow the spell was broken. Holding her away from him, the indigo eyes fastened on her face, he said hoarsely, 'I didn't mean that to happen...I'm sorry.'

Casey found she was staring at the pulse at the base of his throat, a pulse which was pounding as rapidly as her heart. 'S-sorry?' she faltered.

'I haven't touched a woman in a long time—I lost my head.'

'If you lost yours, I certainly lost mine,' Casey said wildly, and then, as his expression hardened, added with sudden fierceness, 'and don't you dare say it's because I feel sorry for you!'

Another wave rudely shoved her towards him. Bryden said tersely, 'Look, can we continue this on dry land? I left my towel over by the rocks.'

Her emotions in a turmoil, Casey led the way across the beach. Bryden shook the sand from his towel and began rubbing his chest in short, hard strokes. 'It was because of the swim,' he said. 'I haven't been able to let go like that for months—that was why I kissed you. I shouldn't have...I'm sorry.'

'I do wish you'd stop saying you're sorry! Because I'm not. I liked it.'

'That's not the point.'

'So what is the point, Bryden?' Casey asked, her eyes glittering. 'That you might risk turning into a real human being?'

'Lay off, Casey.'

She wanted to bang her fists against his chest; paradoxically she also wanted to make him laugh again. But the iron wall of his will beat her back from either course of action. She said with a courage born of desperation, 'What if tomorrow I want to come to the beach your way, Bryden? Am I still forbidden to do that?'

'Of course not—how could I be so churlish after what you did for me today? Hell, Casey, I know I've handled this all wrong . . . I promise if we swim again I won't fall on you like a starving man.' He draped his towel over one shoulder and gave her a crooked smile. 'And in the meantime we'd better go our separate ways.'

It was, rather more politely, another brush-off. Shivering, her flesh covered in goose-bumps, Casey said with a valiant attempt at normality, 'Can you find your way home?'

'Yes. I always put my towel the same distance from the rocks.'

'Goodbye, then.'

'Goodbye, Casey.'

There was something horribly final about the way he said those words. She stumbled across the sand, picked up her belongings and headed for the promontory. In a few short minutes she had gone from an ecstasy she could not have imagined to a pain like the stabbing of a dull knife. And another Casey had emerged: a wanton Casey who would have coupled in the sea with a man she scarcely knew.

CHAPTER THREE

THAT afternoon, when Casey was listlessly washing an accumulation of dishes in the sink, someone knocked on the back door. In a flare of hope she was sure it must be Bryden, for who else did she know in Ragged Island? But when she opened the back door an old man stood on her step. He had flowing white hair, a beard worthy of the Old Testament, and far-seeing grey eyes under brows like crests of foam. 'Simon McIver,' he said economically. 'Come to do the lawn.'

His denim shirt and trousers, faded from many washings, were spotlessly clean; however, his tan would never fade, for it was the kind of tan that came from a lifetime spent outdoors. 'Can I help out?' Casey asked. 'I don't have anything to do this afternoon.'

'You c'n clip.'

And clip she did, hard-pressed to keep up with him as he zipped around the shrubs and trees with the lawn mower. Then she raked while he weeded some of the flower-beds. He would not allow her near the compost pile. 'You got to know how to handle compost,' he said seriously. 'It's temperamental. Like a woman, I guess. If you don't treat it right, you don't get no heat.'

She had to smother a smile, for Simon was in deadly earnest, and the fact that she was a woman did not seem to have occurred to him. 'Have you ever been married, Simon?' she asked.

'Nope.' His eyes sought the jagged rocks of the island offshore, as if it were a loadstone. 'Women want to talk

49

more'n I care for. Never could think of enough things to say to them.'

She watched in dutiful silence while he carefully layered weeds, grass clippings and earth in the compost bin. Then he gave her a sober nod. 'You tell Mrs Draper I'll look after the pruning in a month or so.'

She, Casey, would be long gone by then. 'Is Mr Moore going to stay all winter, Simon?' she blurted.

If he thought her question out of place, he gave no sign. 'Guess so. Yep.'

Hoping she could induce Simon to gossip, she remarked, 'He's like you—he's a loner.'

'Don't talk much, Mr Moore don't. That's true. Well, must be off.' Simon raised his hand in salute with the definite air of a man fleeing a too-curious female, and climbed in his battered old truck. It roared up the driveway, the garden tools rattling in the back like percussion instruments in a band.

Casey went back indoors.

The next morning it rained, a gentle misty rain that under other circumstances she would have enjoyed. But she could not go over to Bryden's in her swimsuit in the rain, and she had no other excuse for going there. She wrote three letters, then walked to the post office to mail them, and on the way back, as though a magnet were dragging her, she turned into Bryden's driveway, her footsteps leaving a silvery trail on the grass verge.

Simon's truck was parked near the house beside the tall cedar hedges. Behind the hedge she could hear the sound of voices, Bryden's deep tones interspersed with Simon's laconic comments. She was about to call out a greeting when she heard Simon say, 'Went to the Drapers' yesterday after I left your place.'

'Oh?' said Bryden. 'Did you meet the young woman who's staying there?'

'Yep.'

'What did you think of her?'

'Good worker,' Simon replied. 'Knew enough to stay away from the compost.'

'High praise indeed,' Bryden commented drily. Then his voice changed. 'Simon, what does she look like?'

There was a puzzled silence. 'OK, I guess. Kinda tall.'

'What colour is her hair? Her eyes?' Bryden persisted.

'Brown 'n' blue,' Simon said promptly.

Through the thick hedge Casey could hear Bryden's exasperated sigh. 'You can do better than that, Simon. Brown like garden soil or brown like the shingles on the house?'

'Oh.' Another silence, during which Casey could picture Simon knitting his brows in unaccustomed thought. 'Well, now, you know that table in your living-room, the one you can see through the window? Mahogany, ain't it? That's what her hair's like. Sort of smooth and polished-lookin'. Shiny, like.'

'And her eyes?'

The silence was shorter this time. 'Her eyes, now that's dead easy. Off Ragged Island, where the water drops to four fathoms, that's what her eyes are like. That green-blue colour, deep, kinda mysterious.' Simon was warming to his task. 'I just figured out what else she reminds me of. My first boat. She was a beauty, that boat, the cleanest lines you ever saw. A proud boat, with a life of her own on the sea. Yet you could trust her in a storm like no other boat I ever had.' Simon sighed. 'It was a sad day, the day I had my last sight o' her. *Lisa-Jane*, I called her.'

'What happened to her, Simon?'

'Lobsters were scarce two seasons in a row. Couldn't keep up the payments.'

'You were never able to buy her back?'

'Guy who bought her sank her a year later in a storm . . . you see, you had to know how to handle her. Mettlesome, she was. Not the boat for everyone.'

'You should have called her *Cassandra-Elizabeth*,' Bryden said.

Casey's cheeks were pink; eavesdropping was not a pastime to be recommended. She crept back along the grass verge, glad of the thickness of the cedars, and heaved a sigh of relief when she reached the end of the driveway. But despite some moral qualms, her heart was singing. Bryden was no more a man to make idle conversation than was Simon. So he must be very interested in her to coax Simon into speech; he had really wanted to know what she looked like. And had got, she thought wryly, remembering *Lisa-Jane*, rather more than he had bargained for.

But the conversation she had overheard gave her the courage that afternoon to take the short cut to Bryden's property. The mist was thicker now, shrouding the trees and muffling the sound of the surf; the prying of its chill fingers around the collar of her jacket made the prospect of swimming out of the question. Perhaps she and Bryden could just talk, she thought optimistically. Around the fire.

However, when she reached the boundary of the trees below his house she discovered that Bryden was not sitting in his living-room in front of the fireplace. Rather, he was jogging in the back garden. Round and round, like a convict in the yard of a prison. He must have been doing it for some time, for the grass was beaten down in a rough square around the circumference of the lawn. Twenty-six paces one way, thirty-three the other, Casey counted, knowing with a sick sensation in the pit of her stomach that he would not want her watching him. This was a private ritual, yet another limitation brought on by his blindness.

But as she turned to go her heel caught in a twig, which snapped with a crack like a whip. Bryden stopped in his tracks and his head turned her way. 'Who's there?' he said sharply.

It never occurred to her to creep away without answering. 'Casey,' she replied, wishing the ground would swallow both the twig and herself.

He walked towards her, his mouth a grim line; he was wearing nylon shorts and a sleeveless mesh shirt, and looked formidably angry. 'You sure have a penchant for spying on me. Do you get your kicks that way?'

'No!'

'Don't tell me you're going swimming,' he added with heavy sarcasm.

He was breathing hard from the exercise, beads of sweat trickling down his chest. Casey said vigorously, 'Bryden, I'm *sorry*. I came over to see if you'd offer me a cup of tea on such a wet day, I had no intention of spying on you. Anyway,' she finished in a spurt of temper, 'that's a horrible word to use, and what are you doing running round and round the garden when you could be jogging properly along one of the back roads? There are miles of dirt roads around here—you don't have to skulk behind your house!'

His own temper flared to meet hers. 'You seem to be forgetting that I have this small problem—I can't see where I'm going. First of all I'd have to find the dirt road, and secondly I'd have to stay between the ditches and out from under the wheels of passing cars. Get real, Casey.'

'You get real,' she retorted. 'I'm not so naïve that I'm suggesting you go alone! Have you made any enquiries in the village? Or in the nearest town? Jogging's the in

thing these days—I know you could find someone to
run with you. But have you even tried, Bryden?'

'No,' he said tightly.

Her temper died. Desperately wanting to touch him,
keeping her hands firmly at her sides, Casey said, 'Just
the other day I read about a blind man who runs in
marathons. He has a regular partner who runs with him.'

As though the words were being dragged from him
one by one, Bryden said, 'I used to run in marathons.'

Somehow she was not surprised that he had competed
in a sport so individual, and, at a deep level, so lonely;
not for Bryden the camaraderie of the baseball team.
She said gently, 'You could run in them again.'

He rubbed the sweat from his forehead with the back
of his hand, his smoke-blue eyes focused above her head.
'Did the partner train with him as well?'

'That's right. As I recall, the blind man was the faster
runner, so it was a challenge for his partner to keep up
with him... Bryden, if the worst comes to the worst,
you pay someone to run with you. I don't think you'll
have to. But it's better to pay someone than to run in
circles around the garden.'

In an expressionless voice he said, 'You sure say it like
it is, don't you?'

'Freedom is what's important,' she answered with
passionate intensity. 'I never go to zoos because I can't
stand seeing the animals run round and round their
cages.'

'So can you run, Casey?'

She gaped at him. 'I jog every other day—but six or
seven miles is my limit. I couldn't run a marathon.'

'Will you take me? Now?'

It was the first favour he had asked of her. Recog-
nising in an instant that she could refuse him nothing,
instantly burying this knowledge deep in her subcon-

scious, Casey said with a radiant smile, 'Sure. Give me ten minutes to go home and change.'

'You have such an expressive voice,' Bryden said quietly. 'It's one of the first things I noticed about you...you're smiling, aren't you?'

'I'm blushing,' she gasped, added, 'Back in ten minutes,' and fled.

It took her no time to change into her shorts and a tank-top, and lace up her running shoes. But then she had to rummage in the back porch for a dog leash she had noticed a couple of days ago: she would use it today to keep her and Bryden together while they ran. She soon found it on a hook beside a raincoat, and for a moment stood smoothing the worn leather in her hands.

Inevitably it reminded her of her job. She had not told Bryden what she did to earn her living; partly because he had not asked, partly because she was afraid that if she did he would interpret her interest in him as professional, himself as just an extension of that job.

Nothing could be further from the truth, she thought unhappily. Bryden interested her simply by existing. And explain that one, Casey Landrigan.

She could not. So she left the cottage, and a few minutes later was back in the clearing. Bryden was stretching out his calf muscles against the side of the house. She went to join him, leaning her palms flat on the cedar shingles, bending first one knee, then the other. 'I love running in the rain,' she said conversationally.

He grunted; he looked as if he was already regretting his impulse. So Casey went through her regular stretching routine in silence, then said, 'I'm ready when you are. I brought an old leash of Susan's—if you hold one end and I take the other, that should keep us close enough.'

She should tell him now, she thought. It was a logical time. But stealing a glance at his impassive profile, she knew she was incapable of saying brightly, Oh, by the way, did I ever tell you that I train guide-dogs? I didn't? How silly of me!

Bryden would not be impressed. One thing at a time, Casey, she adjured herself, and passed him the loop of the leash. He took it without comment.

They went round the corner of the house to the driveway, which was hedged in by the concealing cedars. 'Let's go,' Casey said.

'I'll let you set the pace.'

After they had jogged up the drive, they turned left on to the main highway. Making another effort at conversation, Casey said, 'There's a dirt road we can take a quarter of a mile from here—it goes through a stand of pines and then some open fields, it's very pretty.'

'I know the road,' Bryden said repressively. 'This is my seventh summer at Ragged Island.'

Feeling like a child that had had its knuckles rapped, Casey bit her lip and concentrated on running. She was in good shape, so that once they had turned on to the dirt road her stride lengthened. Bryden adjusted his, and they loped along in silence. Birds chirped in the pines; a tractor growled in one of the fields; a car passed them, the driver plainly noticing nothing out of the ordinary in a pair of joggers on a country road. Insensibly Casey began to relax; it was hard to stay angry and run an eight-minute mile simultaneously.

She glanced over at her companion. He was running easily, his body loose, the tension smoothed from his face. Into her head, perfectly formed, the thought dropped that there was nowhere else in the world she would rather be than here with Bryden.

She increased her pace, not sure how else to cope with this realisation. Smoothly Bryden increased his. They ran on, up a hill, round a curve, past a deserted farmhouse and the ruins of a barn. Twenty minutes later, breathing hard, Casey said, 'I'm not very smart—I figure we've already gone five miles, and we still have to get home.'

Bryden laughed. 'Want to walk for a while?'

'Great idea.' She added, puffing theatrically as they turned around, '*You* could go another ten miles.'

'Seven or eight.'

'Such modesty. Oh, Bryden, don't the woods smell heavenly in September?'

'Tell me what they look like.'

She stood still, marshalling her thoughts. 'Goldenrod and tiny purple asters in the ditches, with scarlet rose-hips tangled among them. Straight ahead of us there's a birch with a silver trunk and lots of gold leaves...like little heaps of coins. Then behind that there's a maple that's starting to turn, its leaves all mottled orange and green.'

'Van Gogh would have loved all those colours, wouldn't he?' Bryden said softly, resting his hands on her shoulders. 'I'm sorry I was rude to you when we started out, Casey. I guess I'm still fighting how dependent I am on others.'

She did not want to be lumped in with anonymous others. 'If you consider it dependency, maybe that's what it turns into. Look at it another way, Bryden—each of us has had an enjoyable run.'

'And it hasn't cost me a cent,' he said fliply.

She flinched away from him. 'Why do you have to spoil everything? Did you think I was going to hold out my hand for ten dollars when we got home? Is that what you thought?'

'No—I'm sorry.' When he tried to pull her closer, he must have felt her resistance. He said harshly, 'I say things like that because I'm afraid of you.'

'Afraid?' Casey repeated blankly. 'Of *me*?'

'Yes. Of you. Cassandra Elizabeth Landrigan. Five feet nine, with hair like polished mahogany and eyes like the depths of the sea—and if you're wondering how I know, I asked Simon.'

Remembering what else Simon had said, Casey stared down at the ground. 'Why did you do that? I didn't even think you liked me.'

'I had to know.' He was smoothing the bare skin of her shoulder with his thumb in a slow, mesmerising rhythm. 'That's what frightens me...there's no element of choice.'

She scuffed at the dirt with her toe. 'That's the way I feel, too,' she confessed.

'I don't believe you! Why in hell would you feel that way?' he said in violent repudiation.

She raised her head, conscious of the cool air on her overheated body. 'Bryden, if we're going to spend any time together at all—and you're committed to being with me for at least the next half-hour—let's get something straight. In a very real way your blindness is irrelevant to me. You just happen to be the most attractive man I have ever met.'

Bryden's expression was inscrutable; she waited for his reply, her breathing still faster than normal. 'Attractive?' he said finally.

'It's not much of a word, is it?' Recklessly, Casey decided to go for broke. 'You're gorgeous. You turn me on. You're the sexiest man east of Ontario.'

Another protracted silence, during which she wondered what on earth had possessed her to speak her mind so plainly. With a strange note in his voice Bryden said, 'You really mean that, don't you?'

'Every word of it.' She gave him an impish grin. 'Once you learn to smile a little more frequently, you'll be fighting the women off.' Not that she particularly cared for that image.

'So does it follow that if I smile at you, I'll be fighting you off?'

She could have discouraged him with a teasing disclaimer; but both he and she deserved better than that. 'Try me,' Casey said.

Bryden's smile took away what remaining breath she had; her knees, which had carried her for five miles without any trouble, suddenly seemed to have dissolved. She said faintly, 'With a high-voltage smile like that, there should be a fence around you. Complete with danger signs.'

His answer was to cup her chin in his hands and find her mouth with his. His kiss began tentatively, as if he was still not quite convinced of her words and was testing their truth; but the softness of her lips, their warmth and instinctive yielding, must have given him something of what he sought. Without haste he took her in his arms, drawing her against the length of his body, enforcing nothing on her, seeking only her own response. One hand was moulding her waist, the other circling her ribs. As her breasts, firm, generously curved, met the hard wall of his chest, his kiss deepened.

Bryden had kissed Casey once before, but that kiss had in no way prepared her for this one, or for the deep joy that welled up within her as he pulled her close. Belonging, she thought in a flash of pure happiness. That was what it was all about. She belonged in Bryden's arms.

She slid her hands around his ribs, exulting in the tautness of tendon and bone; she explored the breadth of his shoulders, her fingers slipping over the sweat-slicked skin; and all the while she was achingly conscious of his kisses. He had been nibbling her lower lip, dropping kisses as soft as flower petals on her cheeks. When he traced the line of her jaw with his mouth, she closed her eyes in ecstasy, loving the roughness of his skin against hers. Then he kissed her closed lids, as if his mouth were his eyes and would delineate her features for him.

But when he sought her mouth again, her lips were parted for the first dart of his tongue, and in the same way that smouldering kindlings burst suddenly into flame her body melted into his and his arms fiercely tightened their hold. Subtlety was lost in raw need. Aware of nothing but a primitive desire for union with this man whose very touch was the stroke of fire, Casey clung to him and moaned his name deep in her throat.

In a rattle of stones, the horn blaring, an ancient half-ton truck careened past them. Bryden broke free, muttering an imprecation under his breath. Almost glad he could not see how two of the three occupants were grinning back over their shoulders, Casey said shakily, 'Just as well—we might have made love on the road.'

'Damn them!' Bryden said with real fury. 'Because I could almost *see* you, Casey—do you know that? The length of your lashes, the sweep of your cheekbones, even the colour in your cheeks . . . and they've taken that away.'

Deeply moved, she could think of nothing to say. Her arms were still looped around his waist. She rested her cheek, which was as flushed as he had suspected, on his chest, trying to catch her breath, and felt his lips on her hair and the pounding of his heart against hers. He murmured, 'So you'd have made love on the road, would you?'

She nodded. For a long moment Bryden was silent; she had no idea what he was thinking. Then, with a trace of laughter in his voice, he asked, 'Are there woods on either side of us?'

Another nod, her forehead moving against his mesh shirt. He said suggestively, 'I could make love to you under a spruce tree. Although it might be a little damp.'

'Very damp,' Casey muttered. 'There's swamp on both sides of the road.'

The laughter rumbled in his chest. 'Can I trust you? Real swamp, with water, peat and mosquitoes? It's not that you've changed your mind?'

'You can trust me, Bryden,' she said soberly.

'Yeah...' With subdued violence he went on, 'You make it all seem so easy, Casey—swimming, jogging, laughing, even making love. All summer I've been like a squirrel on a treadmill, running faster and faster and getting absolutely nowhere. And then you come along...hot-tempered, bossy and so very beautiful.' He stroked her hair with a hand that was not quite steady. 'You're sure Simon didn't lie to me? Your hair's not red?'

'Dark brown,' she insisted, her eyes brimming with happiness.

'Just being able to swim yesterday and run today—I feel like a new man.'

'I noticed,' Casey said pertly.

Throwing back his head, Bryden laughed out loud, the tendons in his neck as strong as rope. 'Despite the fact that we didn't make love in the road, I feel wonderful,' he proclaimed. 'We could get rid of our frustrations by running home.'

'Or we could run to Halifax. It's only sixty miles.'

'You're very good for my ego.'

'Bryden,' she blurted, the words appearing from nowhere she had openly acknowledged, 'are you married?'

'No.'

'Divorced?'

'I've never been married.'

'We haven't talked much about personal things,' she stumbled.

'No.' A shiver ran through his body, as though he was cold. He said restlessly, 'Let's run for a mile or two and walk the rest of the way.'

He had not asked if she was married. Cursing her unruly tongue, for she had totally shattered the closeness between them, Casey led the way across the road so they would face the traffic, and began to run. And, whether it was from sexual frustration or from fear of all the other emotions that were rampaging in her breast, she was able to jog the whole way home. When they finally reached Bryden's house, she passed him the leash. 'You might as well keep this for now,' she gasped.

He took it, slapping it against his palm. 'The weather's supposed to clear tomorrow,' he said abruptly. 'Do you want to swim in the afternoon?'

Casey had been afraid he would not suggest another meeting. Wishing it were today, for she had only two more days left at the cottage, and hoping he could sense neither her relief nor her impatience, she said with assumed casualness, 'Sure.'

'Come to the house, if you like. We'll go down to the beach together. Around two?'

She would have come at five in the morning. Somehow humiliated by this knowledge, she said crisply, 'Fine. See you then.'

'Thank you, Casey,' Bryden said.

She did not want his gratitude. She mumbled something and turned on her heel, wishing she had the energy to run back to the cottage. To run away from Bryden.

The cottage, now familiar to her, welcomed her back. She showered, lay down on the bed and fell asleep.

CHAPTER FOUR

WHEN Casey awoke, she felt out of sorts and extremely tired. She had been crazy to run the better part of ten miles, she thought grumpily. And even more crazy to indulge in lovemaking with a man who was not even interested enough in her to ask if she was married. He probably just wanted an affair, she decided cynically, shutting her mind to the all-too-real emotion Bryden had exhibited. After all, he knew she was only here for another two days. What could be better? Lovemaking, on or off the road, and no commitments. Perfect.

She threw together an omelette for supper, and managed to burn the onions and overdo the eggs. Afterwards she lit a fire in the living-room and picked up her book. But the heroine's very strenuous activities, far too many of which were in bed, did nothing to soothe Casey's nerves. She went back into the kitchen and made a pan of brownies with lots of nuts, covered them with thick chocolate icing and ate half a dozen; she then had a cup of coffee. She read another chapter. She ate two more brownies. At ten o'clock, thoroughly disgruntled and suffering from indigestion, she went to bed.

She must have fallen asleep, for the next thing she knew she was sitting bolt upright in bed with her heart racing. Something had woken her. A noise?

The cottage was wrapped in silence. Slowly Casey relaxed. The noise had probably been part of a nightmare brought on by too much chocolate. She plumped up the pillow and lay down again.

A loud crash came from downstairs, followed by a series of smaller rattles and thuds. Casey sat up again. Her eyes wide, she stared into the darkness. No number of brownies could have made her imagine that. Someone was downstairs.

She had not locked the door when she went to bed. She had not locked a door since she had arrived at the cottage. Wishing frantically that she had, now that it was too late, she wondered what to do. The only telephone in the cottage was downstairs, and no power on earth was going to get her down there.

As if to underline this decision, she heard a sound like breaking glass. More than one person, she thought sickly. A second must have broken one of the windows.

She slithered out of bed, crept to the front window and raised the sash with exquisite care. Then she eased her body through the opening, bruising both elbows as she did so, and crawled out on to the roof of the veranda. The shingles were as rough as sandpaper under her bare feet. Crouched low, she tiptoed to the edge of the roof and peered over.

No one was in sight and the railing on the porch was not that far below. Once she was down, she could run through the woods to Bryden's.

The thought of Bryden gave her courage. Wincing as the edge of the shingles dug into her stomach, she lowered her legs and sought for the railing with her toes, terrified that any moment a shout from downstairs would herald her rather undignified escape. Then her feet felt the smoothness of wood; she rested her weight on the railing, got her balance and leaped to the ground. Bent low, she ran for the trees.

Her brief nightshirt was pale blue, a horribly obvious target. But the thieves must have been busy inside the cottage, for no one yelled at her or burst from the cottage in pursuit of her. Panting with fear, she reached the woods and pushed herself between two young fir trees. The boughs were wet with dew, plastering her shirt to her body. Casey did not care. She stumbled through the woods, making a wide circle of the cottage before daring to emerge on the driveway.

The stones hurt her feet as she scurried along the road, her ears alert for the sound of a vehicle following her; near the highway she cut through the trees to Bryden's driveway, with its tall cedar hedges. Not stopping to think, because if she had she probably would not have had the nerve to go on, she banged on his door and pushed the bell for good measure. If he was a sound sleeper he might not hear her... and then what would she do?

With startling suddenness the door swung open and she saw Bryden standing there, clad in a pair of jeans and nothing else. She ran straight at him, flung her arms around his waist and cried, 'Oh, Bryden, someone's broken into the cottage, or maybe there are two of them. I was so s-scared.'

In an automatic reflex his arms had gone around her. She snuggled into his bare chest and mumbled, 'You feel so solid. And safe. I was afraid you'd be asleep and maybe you wouldn't hear me.'

'I couldn't sleep. Casey, you're shaking like a leaf and you're soaking wet.'

'The trees were wet. So was the grass. Dew, I suppose.'

'You'd better tell me what happened.'

She described the brownies, the mysterious and terrifying noises from downstairs, and her precipitate flight via the veranda, by which time Bryden was grinning. 'It wasn't funny!' she said indignantly. 'I was scared out of my wits.'

'I'm sure you were,' he said, trying to wipe the smile from his lips and not really succeeding. 'You got out of a nasty situation very neatly and I'm glad you came here—even if you are in some kind of a nightgown that's far too abbreviated for my peace of mind. But tell me something else...why the eight brownies?'

She said sweetly, 'To take my mind off you, of course. Why couldn't *you* sleep, Bryden?'

'None of your business.' Very firmly he pushed her away. 'In the closet in my bedroom you'll find some sweatsuits hanging up. Put one on and then we'll go over to your place and see what's going on.'

'By ourselves?' she squeaked.

'We'll case the joint,' he said with another grin.

'You and John Wayne.'

He laughed outright. 'With you as the beautiful heroine who rescued herself rather than waiting for the hero. Off you go, Casey.'

'And what happens if they're still there?'

'We'll call the police. Unless one of them just happens to get in my way. In which case I'll slug him.'

For a moment he looked extremely dangerous. 'You would, wouldn't you?' she said slowly.

'I don't like people who break into houses and scare young women. Particularly if the young woman happens to be you.'

Casey was quite pleased by this last sentiment. 'We should hurry,' she said, 'in case they're vandals.'

'I'm not crawling through the woods with you unless you're properly dressed,' he said inflexibly. 'So move it.'

'Yessir,' said Casey, running for the stairs.

By the time she came down, Bryden had collected a torch, a stout stick, and a shirt, which he was pulling on. He looked very happy. Said Casey, 'You're enjoying this.'

'Are you respectably covered?'

She was inelegantly clad in a sweatsuit five sizes too big. 'I would inspire no one to lust—trust me.'

'It's not you I can't trust. Let's go.'

The journey back to the cottage did not seem nearly as threatening with Bryden at her side, large and imperturbable in the gloom. When they approached the cottage from the rear, it was in darkness, and utterly quiet. 'We'll circle it,' Bryden whispered. 'Try not to make any noise.'

Casey had no intention of making any noise. As they came around the side of the house she breathed, 'The door's open...they must have gotten in that way.' Then she stopped in dismay.

Across the grass, leading to the front door, were two separate trails of footprints in the dew. But they were not human footprints. They were far too small and narrow for that. She followed them to their end, saw where they disappeared under a low-hanging juniper shrub, and said in a choked voice, 'Bryden, I've made a complete fool of myself. There are animal tracks in the grass. One set going to the door and one set leaving.'

In swift comprehension Bryden said, 'Perhaps you only partially latched the door last night?'

Her brow furrowed. 'I could have, I suppose.'

'Racoons,' he said, and again an irrepressible grin tugged at his lips.

She scowled at him. 'Racoons,' she repeated. 'Four-legged fur-bearing animals that live in the woods.'

'And sport black masks worthy of any burglar,' Bryden supplied, now openly laughing. 'I bet he got into your garbage.'

She wailed. 'Will you ever forgive me for hauling you over here in the middle of the night?'

'Let's go in and see if he ate the brownies. If he didn't, you can offer me one and I'll consider the matter.'

They went up the steps, through the open door into the cottage, and then into the kitchen. The metal rubbish bin was tipped on its side, its contents very thoroughly scattered over the floor. Although a glass had been knocked off the counter, the brownies were intact.

'Sit down,' Casey said, 'while I clean up the mess and make you a cup of tea.'

Ten minutes later Bryden was licking chocolate icing from his fingers. 'You're forgiven,' he said blandly. 'Can I have another one?'

She pushed over the plate and wondered why sitting in a disordered kitchen eating brownies should make her feel so wondrously happy. Because Bryden seemed happy too? Was that it? Thoughtfully she took her ninth brownie of the night.

When he had finished his tea, Bryden scraped back his chair. 'I'd better be going,' he said. 'Unless you'd like me to stay, Casey?'

Not sure what he meant, she stammered, 'Oh, I don't think I'll be nervous. Now that I know it was only a racoon.'

'I wasn't thinking about your nerves,' he said.

The width of two chairs was between them and he was making no attempt to touch her. But she now knew exactly what he meant. She blushed, stood up and said, her voice not quite under control, 'I . . . I don't think I'm ready for that, Bryden.'

'Then would you mind walking with me to the end of my driveway?'

There was neither surprise not disappointment in his voice: no emotion at all. Not for the first time Casey had no idea what he was thinking. Had he been hurt by her refusal? Or did he even care? 'Just let me get my sneakers,' she muttered and hurried upstairs.

They walked in silence to his house. At the door Bryden said, 'Two o'clock for a swim?'

'I'm looking forward to it. And, Bryden—thanks.'

'The Great Racoon Rescue,' he murmured. 'It was fun, Casey. See you tomorrow.' And he walked up the steps.

She would have liked a kiss. As she tramped home, she reflected that Casey the intrepid escapee across the veranda roof was not all that brave: she had lacked the courage to kiss Bryden goodnight.

Or did she lack the courage for any consequences of that kiss?

The weather was perfect the next day. Casey and Bryden swam, sunbathed on the sand, and swam again. Then Bryden said, giving her his rare, singularly sweet smile, 'Let's go up to the house. I'll make you a tall, cool drink and we can sit on the patio.'

This sounded like a fine plan to Casey. A few minutes later she was settled on a chaise-longue on Bryden's porch, which overlooked Ragged Island and the ocean; the distant sigh of the waves and the nearer chuckling of the brook fell soothingly on her ears. She took a second sip of the delicious, fruit-laden drink he had made for her and said dreamily, 'It's so beautiful here. I feel very lazy.'

Bryden was sitting beside her in a matching chair. 'No wonder, after chasing burglars all night.'

'It'll be a long time before I make brownies again...you won't be insulted if I fall asleep, will you?'

He stretched out; he was still in his swimming trunks. 'I may do the same. Hard work being John Wayne.'

Casey lay back, the sun caressing her bare arms and legs. Happiness was something she could very easily get used to, she decided just before she fell asleep.

She slept for the better part of an hour. When she woke, she glanced over at the neighbouring recliner. Bryden was still asleep.

She studied his face thoughtfully. With the indigo eyes closed, those eyes that tragically could not see, the rest of his features came into prominence: the dark brows, the decided chin, the slightly crooked nose that gave his face character. Her mother would have thought his hair needed cutting; she, Casey, loved the way it curled around his ears and flopped over his forehead in a thick wave.

A mosquito landed on his cheek. She reached over and brushed it away. Bryden's eyes flew open; he was instantly awake. 'Did you sleep well?'

'You were about to be bitten by a bloodthirsty mosquito,' she explained. 'And yes, I feel wonderful.'

He was smiling at her again, which made her feel even more wonderful. Then her eyes narrowed. 'Hold still,' she said, 'there's that mosquito again.'

She slapped at it, missed, and hit Bryden's ear. He captured her hand, bringing it to his lips. 'Into attacking me, are you?' he murmured, kissing her fingertips one by one.

'If you keep that up, I might.'

'Promises, promises...'

Then he had taken her by the shoulders and was easing her on top of him on the chaise-longue. It creaked alarmingly. Casey said with a breathless giggle, 'We'll fall off.'

'You talk too much,' he said, and stopped her lips with his own.

It was a slow, gentle and infinitely sensual kiss. Achingly conscious of his sun-warmed skin and of the rasp of his body hair against her belly, she kissed him back.

From a long way away she heard him whisper against her mouth, 'Casey, I think you'd better go home.'

'I don't want to.'

'If you don't, we'll end up in bed...will you go to bed with me, Casey?'

She raised her head, pushing back her hair, her eyes searching his face. 'I want to. More than anything. But——'

The chair creaked again. Bryden said, laughter warming his voice, 'We'd better get up. When there's a perfectly good bed available, why make love on a cedar floor?'

Not very gracefully, Casey scrambled to her feet. Bryden stood up too. He let his hands drift up her arms to her shoulders, then bent his head, his mouth trailing kisses along the hollow of her collarbone before dropping lower to discover the warm valley between her breasts. Her body quivered as a poplar leaf quivered at the lightest touch of the wind; she rested her cheek on the silky thickness of his hair, enveloped in sensations all the more powerful for being new to her.

'Come to bed with me,' he said again.

Desperately Casey tried to gather some remnants of common sense. 'Bryden, I—I'm not prepared,' she stammered, unable to be more direct, her cheeks scarlet. 'But quite apart from that, I don't know how I feel about you——'

He said forcefully, 'You want me. I want you. I'll look after the other.'

Feeling as though she were being torn in two, for the Casey of the last twenty-three years had collided head-on with the wild, seductive creature she had become at Ragged Island, she faltered. 'I want you, yes. But there's got to be more to sex than just desire...my mother always said that to go to bed with a man you didn't love with all your heart was to betray something very precious in yourself.'

His face hardened. 'If that's your answer, then you'd better go home.'

His sudden change of mood terrified her. 'Are there no other choices?' she pleaded. 'Why can't we sit here in the sun and talk? Get to know each other better. Or go for a walk on the beach?'

'Because I can't keep my hands off you—that's why! You drive me crazy.'

'I'm not sure that's altogether a compliment, Bryden,' Casey answered, her heart thumping in her breast as she sought to understand the abyss that was suddenly yawning in front of them. 'Maybe it's a cop-out—seduce me so you don't have to treat me like a real human being, so you don't have to talk to me and maybe reveal something of yourself, of your own emotions.' His hiss of indrawn breath told her she was near the mark. 'You're not really afraid of me,' she added in sudden inspiration, 'you're afraid of yourself. And I don't think it's anything to do with your blindness.'

'Since you're so clever, why don't you tell me what I'm afraid of?' he demanded, holding her at arm's length with fingers like claws.

'I can't—I don't know what it is. Although I do know a woman has to be more than just someone you take to bed!'

'You're a born romantic,' he sneered.

Casey was very near tears; from the man who had kissed her so tenderly, he had turned into a cynical stranger. 'If by that you mean that I believe in love— lasting, committed love—then I guess you're right, I am a romantic.'

'You want the world wrapped up in tinsel and pink ribbon, don't you?' he taunted. 'You can't deal with honest lust—you want it prettified, strewn with red roses, enshrouded in love.' He gave an ugly laugh. 'Love...that has to be the most abused word in the English language.'

'Love is important!' Casey cried defiantly.

His words like the flick of a whip, he said, 'So were you lastingly in love with each man you've gone to bed with, Casey?'

Her body seemed to shrink in the cruel grip of his fingers. She had never been to bed with anyone, for the simple reason that she had never been lastingly in love. 'That's a horrible thing to say. I'm not like——'

'Or perhaps you're married and out for a little summer fling?'

Her body dissolving in pain, she tore herself free, knowing she had to get away from his mockery and his ugly accusations that were so far from the truth. 'I'm going home,' she said jaggedly. 'I hate it when you behave like this, Bryden. I hate *you*!'

In her bare feet she ran across the patio. The stairs were a blur; then there was grass underfoot and the welcome shade of the trees. She raced along the path until she came to the cottage, took the steps in two bounds and slammed the door shut behind her, her breath sobbing in her ears. For the first time since she had come to Ragged Island, she turned the key in the lock.

Her last day at the cottage. Casey stood at the upstairs window, remembering how the wind had billowed the curtains on her first day here. There was no wind today. Only a mockingly perfect morning, calm, pristine, exquisitely beautiful.

Inwardly she gave thanks for her rented car. She would leave the cottage right after breakfast and stay away all day. No trips to the beach, no jogging along the dirt roads. No Bryden.

To her surprise she had slept solidly, a leaden sleep that had passed the long hours of the night, even if it had not refreshed her. Nor had it altered in any way her stark view of what had happened yesterday. Bryden was not the man for her: he despised her for believing in love. Bryden thought women were for taking to bed, sexual objects to whom one did not relate in any emotional way; it was so blatantly the classic male chauvinist position that it was almost funny. Almost.

Who are you kidding, Casey? she jeered. It's not funny at all. Meeting Bryden has turned your world upside-down. And do you know why? Because he's made you see yourself as you really are—someone whose sexuality has never been sufficiently aroused to call her moral standards into question. Now that you've met him you'll never be the same again, because through him you've found out you're not at all the person you, and everyone else, thought you were. Calm, even-tempered Casey. Dispassionate, level-headed Casey. Patient, placid Casey.

Her mouth twisted in an unhappy smile. Bryden, certainly, would not apply any of those adjectives to her. Why should he? She had behaved in a way exactly opposite to them ever since she had met him.

And she still had no idea why. He was as far from her image of an ideal man as he could be, for after her father Douglas was her ideal, and Douglas and Bryden were poles apart. Douglas was kind and calm and caring, a man who knew himself and had his life in order. Unlike Bryden.

What was Bryden like? she wondered, gazing unsee-
ingly at the crisp line of the horizon as she recalled all
the clues of the past week. A man of passion, who only
rarely allowed his passion an outlet; a man of fierce
energy and drive, now trammelled by blindness; an independent man, sufficient unto himself, apparently
immune to loneliness. Also, she admitted with reluc-
tance, a man afraid of his feelings. Or maybe she was
glossing over the unpleasant truth that he had no feelings.

What else did she know about him? He was unmarried.
He had had no visitors since she had been here, apart
from Simon. He had pushed her away at every opportunity, yet she would swear that from the beginning he
had been attracted to her.

As a sum total this did not seem very significant com-
pared with all the blanks in her knowledge. She did not
know how he had lost his sight, or how he had earned
his living before he had been blinded. Nor did she know
where he came from, whether he had family, or why he
had never married. These were important facts, she
thought sombrely. The basic coinage of human
interchange.

The other side of that coin was that he knew almost
nothing about her personal life, and had shown very little
curiosity. When she left tomorrow she would at least
know his address and telephone number. He did not even
know where she was from.

The message was clear. He did not care.

Suddenly unable to bear her own thoughts, Casey
whirled around the bedroom gathering her camera and
swimsuit and book, and ran downstairs. The first thing
she did was take the phone off the hook. Then she ate
a quick breakfast, packed a picnic lunch and left the
house.

The garden smelled sweetly of pansies. Not lingering, Casey closed the gate behind her, got in her car and drove off. She turned right so she would not have to pass Bryden's driveway, drove a mile or so, then pulled up and studied the map, soon deciding to take the road along the shore; there were some interesting peninsulas and coves.

The shoreline was both interesting and extremely beautiful, sprinkled with antique and craft shops, and interspersed with charming fishing villages and small, stout white churches. But for all Casey's determination to enjoy herself on this, the last day of her vacation, she was forced to admit by the afternoon that she was only going through the motions. She had found a beach, where she had swum and then eaten her picnic. But it was Saturday, she now realised, and she was the only unaccompanied female on the entire stretch of sand. Beaches were for families and groups and couples.

Especially couples.

She buried her face in her arm, swept by a wave of despair and hopeless longing. I'm going back to the cottage, she thought. I've got to—I have no choice. I'll reconnect the phone and pray that Bryden calls me. And if he doesn't, I'll go and see him this evening. To say goodbye. I suppose I'm being spineless and accommodating and weak-kneed. But I can't leave tomorrow without seeing him again.

She felt minimally better for this decision. After picking up her gear, she went back to the car and headed home; forty-five minutes later she pulled into the driveway and parked in the shade near the cottage. Car-

rying the picnic basket, she fumbled with the latch on
the gate and pushed it open; the hinges squealed.

'Casey?' said a man's voice.

Her head jerked up. Bryden was sitting on the bottom
step.

CHAPTER FIVE

CASEY'S first reaction when she saw Bryden sitting on her steps was pure, uncomplicated joy. He had sought her out. She would not have to leave Ragged Island without seeing him again. But fast on the heels of joy came the memory of how they had parted the day before, of the depth and importance of their misunderstanding.

'Is that you, Casey?' Bryden repeated, getting to his feet.

Clutching the picnic basket to her chest as if it were a shield, her heart thudding like a drum, she slowly closed the gate behind her. 'Yes, it's me,' she said. 'How long have you been here?'

'Ten o'clock this morning.'

It was now four in the afternoon. 'Have you had lunch?'

'I brought some fruit with me and ate that.'

She had been walking towards him. 'You'd better come inside.'

He followed her up the steps and closed the door. Casey put the basket on the counter, heard the low, impersonal hum of the telephone and reached over to put the receiver back on the hook.

Bryden said with no discernible emotion, 'I started calling you at nine this morning. By ten I figured you'd taken the phone off the hook so I came over here. If you hadn't left the door unlocked, I'd have been worried that you'd left for good.'

He could not see her; so why should she be so conscious that all she was wearing was an unbuttoned cotton shirt over her bikini? Her body felt lethargic from the sun; her skin was flaked with salt. She said non-committally, 'I'd gone by nine.'

'When do you go home, Casey?'

'Early tomorrow morning.' Her flight left at eight, so she would have to leave the cottage by five-thirty.

'I don't even know where you live.'

'You haven't asked,' she replied with false calm. They were like two boxers circling each other, she thought fancifully, neither prepared to make the first move.

'I haven't asked anything about you.'

And what was she supposed to say to that? She knew what her Aunt Bridget would say; and with rather over-done politeness said it. 'Would you like to sit down? May I get you a cup of tea?'

'No, thanks. You're not being any help, Casey, are you?'

The first feint. 'I don't see why I should be, Bryden.'

'I suppose not... I came over to apologise.'

'I see,' she said untruthfully.

He took an impetuous step towards her. 'I feel as if I'm talking to a robot. Or one of those dummies in a window display.'

Casey held her ground with an actual effort of will. 'That's because I have no idea what to say to you. Whatever I say seems to be wrong.' With treacherous speed her equanimity deserted her. 'I've never fought with anyone as much as I have with you the last week!'

Two more steps. '*That's* entirely mutual.' With no change in tone he added, 'What are you wearing, Casey? I need to have a picture of you in my mind.'

Her nostrils flared. 'A blue cotton shirt over a bikini. My hair's a mess and I've got sand between my toes. Is there anything else you'd like to know?'

'Now you sound more like the real you,' he said drily.

'I don't know who the real me is any more!' Briefly she closed her eyes, struggling to moderate her voice. 'Bryden, we're getting off topic—you did mention an apology.'

He said flatly, 'Give me your hands.'

She scowled at him in perplexity. His indigo eyes were fastened on her face as if he could actually see her sun-flushed cheeks and tangled curls, and with a pain that pierced her to the core she realised that tomorrow he would vanish from her life.

It seemed more than she could bear. Silently she held out both hands.

He took them in his, enveloping her fingers in his own with a strength he was possibly unaware of. 'I had a long speech prepared,' he said wryly, 'which I had lots of time to rehearse while I was waiting for you. But all I have to do is touch you and it's gone.'

'I don't want long speeches,' she answered with painful honesty. 'I only want to know what you're feeling. Why you're here.'

He said, choosing his words with care, 'You know me well enough, I'm sure, to understand that that's the hardest thing you could ask of me, Casey. Because that's the whole problem—I don't know what my feelings are towards you. Yesterday afternoon it seemed as though the only way to handle them was to take you to bed. I didn't like it when you turned me down—didn't like it at all. I'm sorry for the way I treated you and the things I said to you...although I'd be dishonest to say that I've changed my mind. I still want to take you to bed. My God, how I want to!'

He suddenly brought her hands up to his face, kissing her palms, his head bowed. 'You've been swimming,' he muttered. 'I can taste the salt.'

'I went to the beach at Blandford.' Casey bit her lip. 'I wasn't telling the truth yesterday when I said I hated you, Bryden. I don't hate you. Although I hated the things you said. But I don't understand you, I don't see why you're so afraid of me.' She gave an unconvincing laugh. 'I've never thought of myself as intimidating.'

He let go of her hands, moving his shoulders restlessly. 'I've been alone since I was a boy,' he said. 'You challenge that. You've gotten through my defences, just by being yourself.' His voice roughened with emotion. 'I—I don't even worry much about being blind when I'm with you—it doesn't seem to matter. Heaven knows how you've done that.'

His admission touched her to the heart. Her eyes wet with tears, Casey whispered, 'Bryden, that's the nicest thing you could have said to me.'

He touched her cheek and said huskily, 'You're crying.'

'I guess I am...'

Her tears seemed to loosen his tongue. 'Somehow you seem to understand what it's like to be blind, while at the same time you force me out there into the world to do the things I always used to do. Then the other night when I came over here to punch out the burglars I realised *I* was helping *you*, and not the reverse. You don't know how good it felt, to be of use to someone else— I'd figured my days for that were over.'

He was stroking her salt-tangled hair, each touch of his hand quivering along her nerves. In a small voice she said, 'But yesterday I felt you despised me. Just because I said that love was important.'

'I was angry,' he said slowly. 'Angry and hurt. I'd thought you wanted me just as much as I wanted you. So I wasn't prepared for you to say no.'

In anguish and confusion Casey cried, 'Maybe I was a fool to say no—relying on what my mother said rather than my own feelings.'

He said flatly, 'Whatever is between us is both powerful and elemental, Casey. But it's not love.'

She shivered, pulling away from him. Had she in her heart of hearts hoped he was falling in love with her? 'Let's forget the whole thing,' she said in desperation. 'Because we can't resolve it—we're too different.'

She could see him making a visible effort to follow her lead. 'OK,' he said. 'OK. Which, I guess, brings up the other reason I came here. It's your last evening...will you have dinner with me? Fresh lobster courtesy of Simon, candle-light and wine.'

A potent combination, thought Casey. 'I accept.'

The line of his shoulders relaxed infinitesimally. He hesitated, 'You've already been to the beach. Do you want to go for a run?'

He had spent most of the day sitting in the sun on her step. 'I'd rather go for a swim,' she said quickly.

He smiled at her. 'Great! Why don't you come with me now and I'll change at my place?'

It did not take much to make Bryden happy, Casey thought humbly, following him out of the door. As for herself, she had wasted a whole day when she could have been with him. She must not waste another minute of the little time that was left.

As they descended the steps to the beach, the late afternoon sun was slanting across the sand, the clefts in the headland deeply shadowed, the waves chuckling to themselves. Casey spread out her towel beside Bryden's and grabbed his hand. 'Last one in's a chicken,' she chanted.

'When I was a kid, we used stronger words than chicken.'

'You were a boy,' she said primly, and ran with him into the silvery wash of water on the sand. Again, he soon left her far behind, swimming straight as an arrow towards the horizon; when he returned his face was peaceful, drained of the tension that seemed so integral a part of him.

Casey had been diving for shells. After she had presented him with a rather battered horse mussel, she led the way back up the sand, wringing the water from her pigtail. But when she leaned down for her towel, Bryden reached for his at the same time, and his elbow struck her hard in the ribs. Her gasp of pain was lost in his, 'Casey, I'm sorry! I didn't——' He broke off, then finished bitterly, 'I didn't see you.'

Rubbing her side, Casey said spiritedly, 'People with perfectly good eyesight bump into each other, Bryden. You know that as well as I do.'

'I suppose they do.' He managed a smile. 'Do we need an ambulance?'

'For two broken ribs? Heavens, no.'

He gently squeezed her ribcage. 'I know when you're faking,' he said. Then his voice changed. 'Casey, I'm going to miss you. The beach will be empty without you...'

When he bent his head to kiss her, she responded with a kind of desperation, for in less than twelve hours she would be gone from here and what did her mother's strictures mean in the face of that? His hunger leaped to meet her own; he pulled her against the length of his body, clasping her waist, and in their wet swimsuits they might as well have been naked.

With every nerve in her body Casey felt his hands roam the long curve of her spine and the swell of her hips, and felt, too, his instant arousal. Drowning in a bitter-sweet longing, she kissed him with fierce possessiveness, setting her seal on him, for he belonged to her and she to him, and so it had been from the first moment she had seen him.

She did not resist when he pulled her down to lie with him on the crumpled towels, the sting of sand on her shoulders, her wet hair coiled about her throat. His thigh was thrown over hers; one hand found the fullness of her breast, pushing aside the thin fabric of her bikini to cup her bare flesh.

His body stilled. He said with passionate intensity, 'You're so beautiful, Casey. Your skin is so smooth—like the inside of a seashell.' He raised his head, his eyes a deeper blue than the ocean. 'When I accused you yesterday of coming here for a fling, I knew it was wrong as soon as I said it. You wouldn't do anything like that—cheat or lie. You're too honest.'

Impetuously he buried his face in the hollow between her breasts. She held him to her, and said with careful truth, 'I've never been married or fallen in love with anyone, Bryden. So I've never made love with anyone, either... because I've always believed that love and commitment would have to be part of making love.' He was changing that, but she could not tell him so. 'Unfashionable sentiments, I know, but that was the way I was brought up.'

He raised his head. 'We come from different worlds, Casey. I've always steered clear of women who want commitment. Then, since I was blinded, I wondered if I'd ever make love again... how could I, when I couldn't even see the woman?'

She held him more tightly. 'You can't see me... but does it really matter, Bryden?'

With exquisite sensibility he drew his hand the length of her body, tracing all its curves and concavities. 'It's as though I can see you,' he said huskily. 'As though I know you in a way I never knew a woman before.'

Then, deliberately, he rested his palm on her hip and lay still beside her, dropping his cheek into the hollow of her elbow, tension in the line of his shoulders, his breathing carefully under control. Casey understood immediately that, whatever the cost to him, he would not force her into anything she might regret, even if he was not in sympathy with her reasons. Her heart overflowed with tenderness. Was this the love she had talked about a few moments ago? she wondered. This upwelling of joy mingled with the ache of desire? This absolute certainty that Bryden was the man whom, unbeknown to her, she had been waiting for?

She suddenly felt coolness blanket her skin, and with a thrill of superstitious fear saw that the sun had fallen below the jagged line of spruce trees high on the cliff; their shadows, elongated, sinister, stabbed the sand like black icicles. She had been in danger of forgetting something: Bryden was not in love with her. Did not want to be in love with her.

'You're shivering,' he said in quick concern. Leaving a trail of kisses from her breast to her throat, he gave her a fierce, hard hug, then pulled her to her feet. 'The sun must have gone down.'

'It went behind the trees,' she replied, trying to anchor herself once again in reality. The next sunset she saw would be in Ontario, from her apartment window; a long way from this lonely little beach.

He still had an arm around her, and together they began walking towards the steps. 'Why don't you go to your cottage and have a shower, and then, whenever you're ready, come back to my place?' Bryden said prosaically.

'All right,' she answered in a small voice.

He turned her to face him. 'What's wrong, Casey?'

'You sound so—so ordinary,' she muttered. 'As though nothing's happened.'

'Then I'm a damned good actor,' he said grimly. 'The reason I came to Ragged Island last month was to try and come to grips with the whole issue of my blindness, to figure out what I'd do next. I planned to learn braille. I was going to get on my feet again. Time out. Space to make some decisions.' He gave a short laugh. 'The best laid plans of mice and men . . . because then you arrived, and in just over a week shifted the entire scenario. When I'm with you, I'm not fighting blindness. I'm fighting something else altogether, something much deeper-rooted. Hell, I don't even know what weapons to use.'

'Won't you tell me what you're fighting?' She was almost sure she knew: Bryden the loner had collided with the demands of intimacy. But she also knew he had to share this with her.

He hesitated. 'I don't think I can, Casey—not yet.'

But we have no more time, she wanted to cry. Only tonight and then I'll be gone. 'You can trust me,' she said with a touch of desperation.

'It's not that.' Obviously seeking a change of subject, he patted her arm. 'You're cold, let's go up to the house.'

She had to half run to keep up with him as they crossed the sand. Against the golden sky the tops of the spruce trees looked like witches' hats, harbingers of darkness; there was not a breath of wind, and even the gulls were silent. Fighting for patience, she who was normally never impatient, striving to keep back the questions that wanted to burst from her lips, Casey trotted up the steps and felt the spikiness of grass under her feet. 'Is the dinner burning?' she puffed.

'Sorry,' Bryden slowed down. 'It's my problem, that's what I was trying to say. Something I have to work out on my own.'

'Maybe you do too much on your own.'

'You might have been brought up to believe in all the old-fashioned virtues—but I wasn't,' he answered shortly. 'I was brought up to sort things out by myself. Different strokes for different folks, Casey.'

They had reached the house. The tension was back in his face, she saw with a pang of apprehension. 'I understand,' she said, not altogether truthfully, and gave him a quick kiss on the cheek. 'I'll be back in an hour—I have to wash my hair and it takes a while to dry. Can I bring anything?'

'Yourself,' he answered promptly.

She laughed. 'That's easy! Won't be long.'

Bending down, she pulled on her flip-flops, then padded across the grass. At the edge of the woods she looked back. He was still standing by the back door, his face a pale circle in the evening light. She called clearly, 'See you soon,' and disappeared into the trees.

An hour later Casey was tapping on Bryden's door. She was carrying a bunch of pansies, and the fluttering of her heart was more like that of an adolescent on her first date than a young woman of twenty-three.

The door opened. 'Come in,' Bryden said.

She stepped past him into a large living-room whose windows overlooked the ocean; woven Tibetan mats were scattered on the polished pine floor and Navaho hangings glowed against the stark white walls. The furniture was grouped around a stone fireplace that reached all the way to the cathedral ceiling.

Casey said spontaneously, 'What a beautiful room!' Then, rather breathlessly, 'This is the first time I've seen you formally dressed.'

His shirt was raw silk, full-sleeved with a Cossack collar, tucked into lean-fitting dark trousers; he looked much different from the tousled man on the beach. Hurriedly she added, 'I've brought you some pansies from the garden.'

He took the flowers from her, inhaling their delicate scent before putting them on the plain mahogany coffee-table. A thread of laughter in his voice, he said, 'My turn. So stand still, Casey—I assure you this is purely platonic. I just want to know what you look like.'

She stood very still as he rested his hands on her shoulders. 'You're taller,' he commented. 'High heels?'

'Yes. Turquoise sandals.'

He ran his hands lightly over her body. 'A dress...full skirt, tight at the waist, and——' his voice deepened '—a low neckline.'

'Bryden...'

He kissed the hollow at the base of her throat. 'Your heart-rate's dangerously fast,' he murmured.

'It doesn't know the meaning of the word platonic,' she whispered. 'Nor, I think, do you.'

'Not when I'm within fifty feet of you.' He straightened, his own breathing more rapid, and brushed her earrings. 'Pretty. Gold?'

'Silver and turquoise. My dress has flowers all over it, mostly turquoise, but pink and silver and green as well. My father says I look like a walking rainbow in this dress.'

His touch as delicate as a butterfly's wings, he was exploring her hair; she had piled it high on her crown. 'How do you keep it there?' he asked with genuine amusement.

'Pins and prayer. It's dreadful hair, too fine, so it's always falling all over the place. I had it cut short once, but my brothers said I looked like little Orphan Annie.'

'It feels like satin to me,' Bryden said. 'But I suppose brothers are allowed to make those sorts of remarks.'

'Do you have any brothers or sisters, Bryden?'

'No. Would you like a drink, Casey? Dry sherry or sweet?'

'Dry, please,' she replied, her chin tilting rebelliously. 'I have three brothers, two sisters, four nieces and one nephew, my parents are flourishing after thirty-two years of marriage and I live not far from Ottawa. Where do you come from, Bryden?'

As he passed her a glass of the pale gold sherry, he said evenly, 'Ottawa.'

The liquid rocked in her glass. *Really?*

'Really.' He held up his own glass. 'Should we drink to coincidence, Casey?'

'Indeed,' she said warmly, took a sip of sherry, and sat down on the chesterfield; inwardly she was marvelling that in the vastness that was Canada she and Bryden should come from the same city. Destiny, her heart sang. They were meant to be together. 'How long are you planning to stay here?'

'All winter.'

A little of her euphoria evaporated, for this was only September, and Canadian winters were long. 'By yourself?' she asked.

'That's the idea.'

'But you'll be living in a vacuum!'

He located the chair nearest the fire and sat down himself. 'I'll have lots to do. I have a computer with a braille keyboard, and a machine that transcribes the print in books to either a tape or braille...and I'm paying someone in Ottawa to tape the articles that would interest me in the latest journals. I'm a mathematician, you see, so most of my work is head stuff.'

Knowing she was being far too persistent, but unable to help herself, she said, 'Couldn't you do all that in Ottawa?'

'I needed to get away, Casey. Anyway, I've rented my Ottawa house out for a year.'

This conversation was like a game of draughts, she thought. One gain, two losses. 'Did you lose your sight in Ottawa?'

He nodded. 'The stupidest accident you could imagine,' he said emotionlessly. 'I worked for a think-tank, a mixture of academics, government types and freelance researchers like myself...a good friend of mine is a chemist there. He wanted my advice on some statistical computations, and while we were talking he was showing me some new equipment he'd got.' Bryden tossed back his sherry. 'There was a flaw in a distillation flask. It exploded and I got acid in my eyes. Five seconds either way and I'd have been in the clear.'

Casey could think of nothing to say; the ten feet between Bryden's chair and her own felt like a hundred miles. Or the thousand miles that would be between them by this time tomorrow, she thought wretchedly.

A log tumbled in the fire, shooting sparks up the chimney. Glad to have something to do, she got up and pushed it back with the poker. Bryden said matter-of-factly, 'Enough doom and gloom. I want to know more about you, Casey. Who's your favourite actor, do you read poetry or eat Thai food, what do you think of rock music...that'll do for a start?'

Gamely she rose to the occasion, pushing all thoughts of tomorrow from her mind, and soon she began to relax. Bryden was an imaginative cook, and privately she was impressed by his deftness in the kitchen, which was extremely well organised, with all the ingredients labelled in a raised code. He served a cream of spinach soup he had made the day before, followed by lobster in a brandy cream sauce, salad, and bottled fruit marinated in liqueur. He was an equally accomplished conversationalist, and to her delight she found they had several interests in common.

She carried the coffee into the living-room, and they sat together in front of the fire. 'That was wonderful, Bryden,' Casey said lazily. 'If you ever get tired of mathematics, you could get a job as a chef.'

He laughed. 'I don't think it would be as much fun if I had to earn my living at it . . . speaking of which, I've never asked you what you do, Casey.'

The moment of truth. Casey had rather hoped the subject would not come up; in a vague way she had visualised herself telling him over the phone at some future date. She said with a careful lack of emphasis, 'I'm an apprentice trainer at a guide-dog school near Ottawa.'

There were five seconds of absolute silence. Then Bryden banged his cup down on the table. Coffee slopped into the saucer. 'Guide-dogs? For the blind, you mean?'

'Yes. In eight months I'll be fully qualified.'

His features were taut with anger. 'Why didn't you tell me this before?' he demanded.

'There really wasn't the opportunity——'

'For God's sake, Casey—you should have told me as soon as you knew I was blind!'

'I suppose I should have. But you weren't——'

Again he ruthlessly interrupted her. 'No wonder you understood so well what it's like to be blind; it's your job, after all. So all along I was just an extension of your profession, wasn't I?'

'No!'

He ignored her frantic denial. 'Although if you were on holiday I wouldn't have thought you'd want to spend your time with a blind man. A busman's holiday—isn't that what they call that?'

'Bryden, stop!' she cried, her fists clenched in her lap. 'You're acting as if I were admitting to being a prostitute, for goodness' sake! All right, so I should have told you. But you were as rude as you could be when we first met, and you never did encourage any kind of personal exchange—stop treating me as though I've committed a crime.'

'I thought your interest in me was personal,' he grated. 'Stupid of me, wasn't it? It wasn't personal at all—I was just another opportunity for you to do good. Poor Bryden, I'd better take him swimming and jogging, can't have him sitting around feeling sorry for himself, that's bad psychology—what are you, a kind of Florence Nightingale for the blind? An off-duty Pollyanna?'

Casey stood up in a flurry of skirts. 'You're twisting everything,' she said furiously. 'It *wasn't* like that. I really liked you. For yourself.'

'Oh, sure,' he sneered. 'I'm just surprised you didn't put the move on me to get a guide-dog. Shouldn't you be out drumming up some business?'

'I don't have to stand here and listen to this,' Casey blazed. 'I'm leaving and I——'

In a flash of movement he grabbed her wrist, his fingers wrapping around it like a manacle. 'You're not going anywhere until we have this out,' he said grimly. 'Because I'm beginning to realise something else. This was all arranged, wasn't it? Not coincidence at all.'

'What *are* you talking about?' she said, futilely trying to tug free.

'Susan Draper is a cousin of yours. She's also a friend of my next-door neighbours in Ottawa—Jenny and Matthew Sibley. Do you know the Sibleys?'

Puzzled, Casey searched her memory. 'I know who they are, yes. I met them some time last spring, at a party at Susan's house. Although I talked to Jenny more than her husband. So what, Bryden?'

'So this *was* a set-up. I can hear it all now—you and Jenny and Susan sitting around having a cosy cup of coffee and thinking what a great chance to improve Bryden's life—get him involved with a guide-dog trainer. A pretty one into the bargain. Jenny always was thrusting stray females under my nose.'

With dangerous calm Casey said, 'Are you suggesting I deliberately came down here to get to know you?'

'That's exactly what I'm suggesting.'

'Do you realise what that implies,' she seethed. 'It implies I lied to you right from the start.'

'I never did have much faith in coincidence.'

Casey fought for breath, angrier than she had ever been in her life, and at a deeper level terrified out of her wits. Through gritted teeth she said, 'Susan phoned me and offered me her cottage. I had a week's holiday coming up and jumped at the opportunity. Your name was at no time mentioned.'

'And then you just sort of forgot to tell me that you work with blind people all year round,' Bryden jeered. 'Forgive me if I have trouble with that story, Casey.'

'It's not a story—it's the truth,' she cried. 'And please let go of my wrist, you're hurting it.'

He dropped it as if it were a poisonous snake. 'Why don't you get the hell out of here?' he snarled. 'And when you get home, tell Jenny and Susan to mind their own business. I don't need a woman any more than I need a dog.'

The world lay in ruins around her feet. Casey said flatly, 'I doubt very much if you'd get one—a dog, that is. You have to be capable of loving a guide-dog, of bonding to it . . . I don't think you're capable of loving anything or anyone, Bryden, you're too busy protecting yourself. You've got all your emotions safely under lock and key and that's where they're going to stay.'

'So that's what you think, is it?' With that swiftness of movement that was so unexpected, he seized her by the elbows, hauled her towards him, and kissed her with bruising strength on the lips. It was a kiss compounded of fury and frustration, and when it was over he pushed her away so violently that she staggered. 'Get out of here, Casey, before I do something I'll regret.'

'Like listen to me?' she flashed.

'Like take you to bed.'

Unconsciously she backed off a step. With raw truth she said, 'I wouldn't go.'

'Then what are you waiting for?'

What *was* she waiting for? A miracle, she thought frantically. 'Bryden, we can't part like this——'

The words burst from him. 'I was starting to trust you. To believe you represented something new in my life, something other people seem to take for granted that has always been out of my reach.' He laughed, a laugh that shivered along her nerves. 'So much for trust. So much for emotion. I was a blind fool, Casey—which has nothing to do with the fact that I can't see you.'

Grasping at straws, she said, 'I'll get Susan to write to you, to explain. Or Jenny.'

'Please don't bother. Just go, will you?'

Out of sheer desperation she made one last stand. Gathering the remnants of her dignity, she said, 'This is wrong, Bryden. What we're doing is wrong.'

He said nothing, simply standing statue-still waiting for her to leave; there were lines carved in his face like the crevices in the cliffs. Her throat raw, she whispered, 'A couple of hours ago you told me I was honest, that I wouldn't cheat or lie.'

'I was wrong.'

Casey made a tiny, pleading gesture with one hand, then let it fall helplessly to her side. 'There's nothing more to say then, is there? I—take care of yourself.'

She could not bear to say goodbye. Rounding the end of the mahogany table, the table that was like the colour of her hair, she walked steadily to the door, her heels clicking on the floor. She opened it, passed through, and closed it quietly behind her. Only then did she start to run.

The woods enveloped her. With the agility of a deer Casey raced along the path, her breath sobbing in her throat, her skirts swirling about her legs. She knew exactly what she was going to do. She was going to pack her things, clean up the cottage, and drive to the airport tonight. She would rather spend the night on a bench in the terminal than next door to Bryden. Bryden, who believed her capable of deliberate deceit. Bryden, who had not believed her when she had spoken the truth...she never wanted to see him again, she thought, almost falling up the steps of the cottage.

You never will, Casey, a mocking voice whispered in her ear.

She stumbled upstairs and threw her suitcase on the bed. But then something drew her to the window that overlooked the cedar and stone house of her next-door neighbour. She stared across the tops of the trees, which stood unmoving like sentinels around his property. The beauty of the starlit night caught at her heart.

The house was in darkness. The darkness that Bryden had chosen...

At the first opportunity after she got home, Casey phoned Susan and arranged to return the key of the cottage. She wanted it out of her possession, for it was too tangible a reminder of Bryden. Once she was rid of it she would start to forget him, she thought, as she rang Susan's doorbell. She had to. Because remembering him hurt too much.

Susan, who had long black hair and a tranquil disposition, ushered her indoors. 'The coffee-pot's on,' she said, leading Casey into the kitchen.

Jenny Sibley was sitting at the round maple table.

Casey stopped in her tracks and said levelly, 'So Bryden was right—it *was* a set-up.'

Jenny's lashes flickered. 'Hello, Casey. Good to see you again.'

Casey had only met Jenny once, but she was not in the mood for social niceties. 'You're the one who suggested to Susan that she lend me the cottage,' she accused. 'Knowing Bryden would be next door.'

Jenny tossed her head and said defiantly, 'Yes, I did— I thought you were just the person Bryden needed. So today, when Susan mentioned you were bringing the key back, I invited myself over to find out how you got along.'

Susan passed Casey a mug of coffee and said pacifically, 'Did you like the cottage, Casey?'

'Oh, I loved the cottage,' Casey replied, her eyes pools of brilliant turquoise as she threw the key on the table. 'But you might at least have told me you had a neighbour who was blind.'

'Jenny persuaded me not to. She thought it would be more natural if you didn't know. Here's the cream, Casey—do you take sugar?'

Casey, perforce, pulled out a chair and accepted the cream jug. She said with painful accuracy, 'Bryden thinks the three of us sat down just like this and plotted my holiday. All for his own good, of course.'

Jenny scowled. 'You mean he was angry?'

'You might say so.'

'But you straightened it out before you left,' Jenny said hopefully.

'We parted on the mutual understanding that we would never see each other again.'

'You didn't *like* each other?' Jenny cried.

'I didn't say that.' Casey picked up her mug with both hands so no one would see that they were trembling; meanly, she was rather pleased that Jenny was suffering a little.

'We should have been straightforward, Jenny,' Susan put in.

'But then Casey wouldn't have gone...would you, Casey?'

'Probably not!' Casey snapped. 'And we'd all have been better off.'

Susan said with genuine concern, 'You certainly don't look very rested.'

As Casey knew all too well, she looked dreadful; a lavish amount of make-up had not been able to hide the circles under her eyes. 'You fell in love with him!' Jenny exclaimed, with a lack of tact excessive even for her.

'I did *not*,' Casey retorted, and stared hard into her coffee so she would not cry.

'You're really angry with me, aren't you?' Jenny moaned. 'But I acted for the best, Casey. I was *worried* about him all alone there in the middle of nowhere and

I hoped you'd at least bring him back to Ottawa where he belongs, and I really liked you that one time I met you, so I thought *he* would too.' She bit into one of Susan's muffins, looking on the verge of tears herself; Jenny liked to be liked. 'Matthew warned me not to interfere,' she finished dolefully.

Casey gulped down her coffee, wishing Jenny had paid more attention to her husband. 'Well, it's done now,' she said. 'Over and done with,' and heard the words like a knell on her heart.

'I'll phone him and explain!'

'Please don't. He wouldn't believe you.' With an immense effort Casey managed to pull herself together. 'Your cottage is beautiful, Susan. By the way, Simon cut the grass while I was there and said he'd look after the pruning.'

'Simon's a gem,' Susan responded, patently glad to discuss someone other than Bryden, and rambling on long enough for Casey to finish her coffee.

Casey stood up. 'I can't stay, I've got the school van and several more errands to run. I'm sorry if I was rude, Jenny... and thanks again for the cottage, Susan.' With a falsely bright smile that included them both, she headed for the door. And as she drove to the school she told herself, over the rattle of dog cages in the back, that the episode at the cottage was now finished. All that remained was to forget the man with the indigo eyes who, in bringing her body to life, had also become entangled in her emotions.

He was in the past. He had no place in her future.

March was at its worst, loud, blustery and importunate. The windows of the conference-room looked over the kennels, behind which were fields where dirty snow lay in the furrows and the maples stretched their frozen limbs to a leaden sky. Casey laughed. 'It can only get better,' she said.

The glasses slipped a little further on the director's long nose. 'Douglas, who have you got lined up for us?'

Douglas shuffled his papers; his eyes, grey as the sky, were lit with enthusiasm. 'Four students, two from the west coast near Vancouver, and two from the east, one from New Brunswick and one from Nova Scotia. On the basis of the interviews I've tentatively matched them with the dogs: two for Casey and two for me. Here's the sheet.' He passed one to David Canning and one to Casey.

All prospective students were interviewed in their homes; Douglas had done all the interviews for this class because Casey had been tied up training dogs and doing some publicity work around the province. Without the slightest premonition that any of the names on the list would mean anything to her, she scanned it, wondering which dogs Douglas had chosen. At least three that she had been training for the last six months were ready for a client; she ran her eyes down the page.

The name of the fourth person leaped out from the paper. Bryden Moore.

Totally unprepared, she dropped the paper. It skidded off the table on to the floor. Douglas leaned over to retrieve it, passing it to her with one of his good-natured grins. Then his brow creased with concern. 'What's wrong, Casey? Don't you feel well?'

The colour had drained from her face and her eyes were blank with shock. The sight of Bryden's name on a piece of paper, the knowledge that he would be arriving here in just over a week, had horrified her. 'I'm fine,' she said shakily, and knew she would have to tell the truth, or, at least, an edited version of the truth. 'I've met Bryden Moore. Last September. We didn't exactly hit it off.'

David Canning frowned. 'That's unfortunate. I notice, though, that he's matched with one of Douglas's dogs. Did you know about this, Douglas?'

'No,' said Douglas. He too was frowning at her.

Casey had told no one other than Jenny and Susan about the débâcle of her holiday at the cottage. She said defensively, 'You were away when I came back to work last fall, Douglas. Anyway, I never expected to see him again—why would I mention him?'

'What do you mean by not hitting it off?' Douglas asked in an unfriendly voice.

'His house was next door to Susan's cottage. We just...argued a lot,' she finished weakly.

'You know the rules, Casey,' David Canning said evenly. 'Absolutely no involvements of a personal nature between students and staff.'

'This happened six months ago. There's been no contact since then,' she said defensively. Nor had there been. At first every telephone call and mail delivery had caused her heart to beat faster in the hope that she would hear from Bryden; but as autumn had faded into winter and Christmas had passed she had gradually given up hope.

The director nodded. 'Fine. I'll depend on you to treat him the same as you treat the other three students. Now, Douglas, you've put Bryden Moore with Caesar and the other man with Maggie...what's the rationale?'

The conversation became technical, revolving as much around canine psychology as human, and Casey knew the subject of her relationship with Bryden would not be referred to again. Providing, she thought with a quiver of fear, she obeyed the rules.

She forced herself to pay attention. Her two dogs, Bess and Dan, had been allocated to the two female students, Marsha and Carole; she listened carefully, because the matching of the dogs to the students was a critical part of the process. The meeting did not last long, for David Canning put a lot of faith in the judgement of his trainers and rarely questioned their decisions. Pushing back his chair, he said, 'All four people arrive Monday afternoon, then. The usual briefing that evening in the lounge,' gave them his deceptively vague smile and ambled out of the room.

Quickly Casey stood up. But before she could follow him, Douglas said, 'I still think it's funny you didn't tell me about meeting Bryden Moore. He is blind, after all.'

'When you interviewed him, did he tell you about meeting me?' she retorted.

His eyes narrowed. 'No. So am I supposed to believe it's coincidence that he's turning up at the school where you happen to teach?'

Coincidence. She hated that word. 'I have no idea what's going on in his head,' she said shortly. 'All I know is that I have had no contact with him whatsoever since last September.'

Douglas also stood up, making rather a business of gathering his notes. 'This puts me in an awkward position,' he said gruffly. 'I'm sure you know how I feel about you, Casey. But you also know I can't do anything about that until your apprenticeship is over; it would be highly unprofessional.'

Since last September Casey had not been so sanguine that she and Douglas would drift into any kind of relationship, particularly the one she had always envisaged: comfortable, friendly, adding a dimension to her life without in any way disturbing its tenor. Bryden had killed that dream. With Bryden she had discovered the meaning of passion, and the lesson could not be unlearned.

She fumbled for words, for how did one refuse a proposal that had not been made? 'I don't know what I want, Douglas,' she said as honestly as she could. 'Can't we just leave it for now?'

'We don't have much choice, do we?' he said with a glimmer of the smile she so much liked. 'What are you up to today?'

'I thought I'd take Dan, Bess and Barney into the city and do some on-kerb obstacle work.' She was having a slight problem with Barney; she began to discuss it as they went downstairs, and the day slipped into its normal routine.

Because Casey's job was demanding, the week before the arrival of the students passed more quickly than she wished. She was delegated to meet the two students from the west, who were arriving on the same plane; Douglas connected with the flights from the maritimes later in the day. So Casey was in the student lounge at the school chatting to Carole and Hartley and trying very hard to ignore her watch when Douglas finally ushered two people in the door. Determined that none of her inner turmoil would show, Casey calmly finished her sentence and stood up.

'Marsha, this is Casey Landrigan,' Douglas said. 'Casey's our other instructor...Marsha McMillan, Casey.' Casey shook hands, murmuring commonplaces. 'And Bryden Moore...I believe you two already know each other.'

Bryden looked fit and handsome, his face tanned, his bearing relaxed; he did not look as if he had been pining for her all winter in the way she had pined for him. 'How are you, Bryden?' Casey said politely. 'You certainly look well.'

Holding out his hand, he said in the deep voice she remembered so well, 'I took your advice and found someone to run with. We're training for a marathon in July.'

When she took the proffered hand in her own, she discovered instantly that nothing had changed: the strong clasp of his fingers brought back memories that had lain dormant for months. Furious with herself and very much aware of Douglas listening to every word, she said, 'I was surprised to find out you were coming here—I hadn't expected to meet you again.'

He said casually, 'Hadn't you? But you're the one who initially gave me the idea of a guide-dog.'

Remembering with embarrassing clarity the very words she had used, Casey took refuge in formality. 'Welcome to the school...Marsha, how was your journey?'

She was never to remember what she said or did for the rest of that day; somehow she got through it without singling out Bryden in any way and thereby disgracing herself. After dinner, served in the oak-panelled dining-room, they all moved back to the lounge, where in front of a cheerful log fire David Canning described the daily routine for the next month. 'Two days of harness work before you get your dogs,' he finished. 'I know you're all anxious to meet your dogs, but we have to satisfy ourselves that we've made the best match possible. Any questions?'

Inevitably there were. But by nine-thirty Casey was driving home to her apartment in the nearby village of Humbertsville, more tired than she had been for months. She was also suffering from an acute sense of anti-climax: she had met Bryden again after nearly seven months and absolutely nothing had happened.

What did you expect, Casey? she jeered. That he'd fall on you in front of everyone? That *would* finish your prospects at the school. Just be grateful he's not one of your students and stop thinking about him.

Like most advice, this was easier said than done. She watered her plants, wrote cheques out for a couple of bills and went to bed.

For the next two days Casey worked extremely hard with Marsha and Carole; then she, Douglas and the director had an early morning meeting in the conference-room. Douglas said soberly, 'There's a problem. I don't think Bryden's suited to Caesar. The man's got a lot more sensitivity of touch than I'd realised—he'd be much better with a dog like Bess.'

With a horrible sense of inevitability Casey said, 'Marsha's too heavy-handed for Bess.'

'Easy,' said David Canning. 'Switch them.'

For several minutes they discussed the consequences of this. Then the director said, 'You'll be all right with that change, Casey? You don't seem to be having any problem with Bryden.'

'I'll be fine,' she said fatalistically. She had to be. The job that she loved depended on it.

'I'll tell him,' Douglas said.

'Good. Give them the dogs this morning, let them spend an hour or so together in their rooms, and then start the training this afternoon,' David Canning said, pushing his glasses towards the bridge of his nose. Promptly they slid down again. 'I'm off then. Good luck.'

She would need it, thought Casey with grim humour as she vanished into her little office to look after the necessary paperwork. Then she went to the kennels and led Dan, a blunt-nosed Labrador retriever, to Carole's room, where she introduced the dog to her and stayed a few minutes to make sure they were comfortable together. Carole had waited a long time for this moment, and as always Casey was touched by the initial meeting of the dog and its blind human partner.

She walked back to the kennels, hunched in her jacket. Bess was a favourite of hers, and as she clipped on the white leather harness Casey said her private farewell to the dog, for from now on she must back away so that the all-important bond between Bryden and Bess developed as it should. She and the dog walked briskly to the house and down the corridor where the student rooms were located. She tapped on Bryden's door. 'It's Casey.'

'Come in.'

Bryden was sitting on the bed, dressed in grey cords and a blue sweater. Casey said, 'I've brought your dog, Bryden. Her name's Bess—she's a golden retriever who's almost two years old. She'll need firm handling, because she can be strong-willed, but on the other hand she also needs a lot of affection because she's very sensitive...I'm sure you'll get along well together.'

When she led the dog over to him Bess sniffed his hand, her tail wagging. Bryden rubbed the dog's forehead, his face set. 'Thank you,' he said.

Clearly he wanted her to be gone. Casey said with a serenity she was far from feeling, 'Her coat is beautiful, all shades of gold and chestnut...after lunch, we'll go out for the first walk.'

She left his bedroom and marched to the grooming-room, where she checked some supplies, making rather a lot of noise about it. This month could be a definite test of character; if she could maintain her equanimity with Bryden, she could work with anyone.

Her equanimity was put to the test that very afternoon. The first walk was along the pavement from the school to the village and back again. Casey took Bryden and Bess first, adjusting Bryden's gloved hand on the harness, explaining to him how the dog had been trained to walk in a straight line. As soon as she had finished, he said, 'Is there anyone else here?'

'Douglas and Marsha are just ahead of us.'

The wind ruffled his hair. 'When will I get the chance to talk to you alone?'

'You won't.'

'A month is a long time, Casey. We'll be alone sooner or later.'

'This isn't Ragged Island, Bryden,' she said steadily. 'Here, I'm your instructor, and any conversation between us relates only to the course.'

'We'll see about that,' he said in a steel voice. 'Now, where are we going?'

Casey bit her lip. What had he wanted to say to her? And why did he have to be alone with her to say it? 'We'll walk to the village,' she said, and carefully went over the commands he might need.

Casey's character was tested more than once during the next week. But she was calm, friendly and supportive with both Carole and Bryden as she took them and the dogs through their paces in straight-line walks, right and left turns, kerb work and obstacles; her voice, she was proud to notice, was no different whether she was with one or the other.

When they worked together Bryden listened carefully to everything she said and rarely forgot any of her instructions, and he was unfailingly polite. There was only one area in which Casey could fault his efficiency: at least twice a day she would have to remind him to praise Bess, to pat her and tell her she was a good dog. He would immediately do so. But it was at best a mechanical performance; his heart was not in it.

Casey could not help remembering the words she had flung at him about love and bonding, words that were proving more accurate than she cared for. However, she did not yet share her concern with Douglas, for there were three weeks left in the course and most problems surfaced in the early days. Neither did she share with him or with anyone else how much it was costing her in terms of emotional energy to spend so much time with Bryden. He, apart from that initial outburst, did not seem the slightest bit affected by her.

That this was not the case Casey found out one crisp morning the second week of the course, when a free run was scheduled. To the right of the kennels was a fenced paddock; she and Bryden went there alone half an hour before lunch. She described the latch on the gate and waited until he had locked it behind them. Then she said matter-of-factly, 'There's no one else here, so there aren't any distractions for Bess. Next time we have a free run Carole and Dan will be here, too, which will make it much more of a challenge. The idea is——'

Bryden interrupted her. 'Are you telling me we're alone?'

'Yes. But——'

Again he ruthlessly overrode her. 'No one in sight?'

'That's correct,' she said frostily. 'It's best for the dog to——'

'The dog can wait. Do you realise this is the first time in ten days that you and I have had five minutes to ourselves?'

She did. All too much. She said disagreeably, 'The object of this course is not for you and me to exchange pleasantries.'

'Are you engaged to Douglas?'

Her jaw dropped. 'No!'

'Then what the hell's wrong with you? Ever since I came here you've been acting as if we'd never met before. Let alone nearly made love in the middle of a dirt road...you hadn't forgotten that, had you, Casey?'

'That's in the past, Bryden. *You* were the one who kicked me out of your house—or have you forgotten that?'

'I made a mistake,' he said stiffly.

'And it took you six months to realise it?'

'No. A great deal less than six months.'

'Too bad you hadn't bothered to let me know.'

'I applied to the school instead.'

It was not the answer she had wanted. Casey cast caution to the wind. 'So are you here to get a guide-dog or to pester me? Because if it's to pester me, you've come to the wrong place!'

'To get a dog, of course—I need to be more independent. But I also had to see you again, Casey. It's been hell the last ten days—I can't even stop dreaming about you, for God's sake!'

He looked more angry than loving. But he had grabbed her sleeve, and she had no idea what he might do next. Horribly aware that the old Tudor house had at least twelve windows overlooking the paddock, and that it would only take David Canning looking through one of them to ruin her reputation, Casey took a deep breath and said with icy calm, 'Let's get something straight right now, Bryden. My job's at stake here. There's one inviolable rule at this school—no personal involvement of any kind between students and staff. I'm almost at the end of my apprenticeship...three years of hard work. I'm not going to jeopardise that just so you can kiss me in the paddock.'

His jaw taut, Bryden demanded, 'Is that why you've been treating me like a complete stranger?'

'You are a stranger to me, Bryden... September was a long time ago and is better forgotten. But you're also one of my students, and in case you hadn't noticed I've been passing on a lot of hard-earned knowledge so that you and Bess will be a successful unit. That's my job. That's what I'm paid to do.'

'So to you I'm one half of a unit? No different from Carole or Marsha or Hartley?'

'That's right, Bryden,' she said, and knew that she was lying.

'I see.' He let go of her arm, his face an inscrutable mask. 'Then we'd better get on with this free run, hadn't we? As that's the only reason we're here.'

By a monumental effort of will Casey voiced none of the questions beating in her brain. Are you sorry you kicked me out? Do you still believe the whole visit was a set-up and that I wilfully deceived you? Instead she said in a colourless voice, 'We use a different collar for free runs, one with two bells on it so you can hear where Bess is. You call her back with this whistle.'

The lesson proceeded. Bess had a marvellous run, and Bryden, on the third attempt, coaxed her back to him. But afterwards, when they went to the dining-room for lunch, Bess was the only one who looked happy.

Even Bess did not look happy the following day. The lesson was on near and far traffic; Douglas, driving his car, purposely set up situations in which Bess, trained to step out into the road at Bryden's command, was now required to disobey in order to protect her master. It was a difficult lesson; Bryden was tense and Bess balky. To make matters worse, the weather seemed in conspiracy against them, the wind raw and a fine, freezing rain stinging their faces.

Eventually Casey said, 'OK, let's call it quits. This session is hard on the dog, Bryden, because she has to go against the rules. So she needs lots of praise. She can feel your tension too—try and relax.'

Bryden blew on his cold fingers rather than bending down to pat the dog. Casey sighed. She was increasingly afraid that she and Douglas had not made the right match after all, for Bess needed far more affection than Bryden seemed capable of giving. You can't legislate love, she thought unhappily, walking twenty feet behind Bryden as he and Bess started back along the suburban street towards the van.

Because the ground was uneven, the paved driveways that led from the pavement to the neat brick houses were on a steep upward slope; as Bryden approached one of these driveways, a long blue car came rolling down it in neutral, its engine silent. Bess stopped, sitting down.

'Forward!' Bryden ordered.

The car was no more than four feet away from them. Bess stayed where she was. 'Hup-up!' Bryden said even more sharply, giving an exaggerated hand signal, his whole bearing fraught with tamped-down anger.

The engine roared into life. With a screech of tyres the car pulled out on to the street. Bryden's head swung to the left to follow the sound, the colour seeping from his face. Casey said quietly from behind him, 'Bess stopped because she saw the car coming. Otherwise you would have walked right in front of it.' And then she waited to see what he would do.

He closed his eyes, his shoulders sagging. 'That car was for real—nothing to do with Douglas?'

'Douglas went back to the van five minutes ago.'

'I'd have gone right into it.'

She said nothing. His face still very pale under his wind-tangled hair, his red ski-jacket a bright patch of colour, Bryden knelt down on the wet pavement. Awkwardly he put his arms around the dog. 'Thanks, Bess,' he said huskily. 'Good girl . . . good dog.'

Bess wagged her tail and licked his nose. For a moment Bryden rested his cheek on her silky hair, his face convulsed with an emotion so strong that Casey averted her eyes. Then he stood up, picked up the harness handle again and said, 'Forward, Bess.'

A lump in her throat, her mind full of questions, Casey trudged along behind them to the van, where Carole was waiting her turn. When they eventually arrived back at the school everyone was tired. The students and dogs headed for the grooming-room; Casey got herself a coffee in the kitchen, drank it staring out of the window at the stripped oak trees, then walked down the hall to the grooming-room herself to see how the feed was holding out. The room was not, as she had expected, empty; Bryden was sitting on one of the wide benches, Bess beside him. He was brushing the long golden hair on the dog's flanks, an expression on his face Casey had never seen before.

'I'm sorry—I didn't realise you were still here,' she said.

'Casey?'

The expression was gone, the face closed. 'Bryden,' she said, 'did you ever have a dog before?'

As he got to his feet Bess jumped to the floor, shaking herself. 'What business is that of yours?' he said curtly.

'I wondered. That's all.'

He picked up the brush and comb. 'I had a puppy once.'

Casey stared at him, all her senses alert. 'What happened to it?' she said softly.

'My father thought I was growing too fond of it. He had it destroyed.'

In a shocked whisper she said, 'That's terrible, Bryden!'

'The puppy was really the housekeeper's. She smuggled it into the house and I used to play with it after school.'

'I don't understand how he could do that!'

'He believed in all the Ernest Hemingway stuff, the macho virtues, the strong silent men who had no use for women or the gentler emotions. Animals, according to my father, were to be hunted. Not kept as pets.'

'It must have broken your heart,' Casey said, entirely without hyperbole.

His mouth thinned. 'I was only six, but I already knew better than to cry in front of my father.'

It was the kind of story that revealed far more than it described. Casey rested her hand on his sleeve. 'Is that why it's been so difficult for you to give Bess any affection?'

He shrugged free and said irritably, 'Quit psycho-analysing me, Casey.'

She was sure she was right. She was also sure she would get no more confidences out of Bryden today. 'It's nearly suppertime,' she said casually. 'So I'd better check the feed in case I have to get more from the kennels. Excuse me, will you?'

As she turned away he put the brush and comb in his locker and left the room. Gazing at the heaped sacks of dog food, her face very thoughtful, Casey knew she had been given her first real clue to the mystery that was Bryden.

CHAPTER SEVEN

BECAUSE the weather was still bitterly cold the following day, Douglas decreed they would do some inside work in one of the Ottawa malls. Casey took Carole and Dan first, putting in an hour and a half's intensive work with them, finishing with a short bus ride back to the van; then she said cheerfully, 'Your turn, Bryden. Got your gloves? You're going to need them.'

They left the van, which was parked on a quiet side-street, and turned on to Rideau Street. Pneumatic drills clattered from a construction site; buses roared around the corners; horns blared and pedestrians jockeyed for position at the traffic lights. Bryden, Casey was pleased to notice, took his time at the lights, listening carefully to the direction of the traffic before ordering Bess to leave the kerb. As they threaded their way along the wide pavement, she kept up a soft-voiced commentary. 'Bess took you to the left there to avoid a display rack...she's hesitating because three women are blocking the way...the door straight ahead of you opens towards you...'

A bunch of teenagers, their ghetto blaster at full volume, jostled Bryden as he passed through the doors into the mall. The air smelled warm and stale. Muzak assailed their ears. They negotiated two flights of steps; they went down on a crowded escalator; they went into a shop so Bryden could purchase some razor-blades; and through all this noise and confusion Bess threaded her way, head up, ears pricked.

When he had walked out of the shop, Bryden stood for a moment, a tall, commanding figure in his ski-jacket and cords. 'I need to go left to find the stairs again, don't I, Casey?'

'Correct! You've got a fabulous sense of direction,' she teased. 'I often get lost in here.'

But he was not listening. A strange expression on his face, he said, 'And then Bess will show me where the first stair is, and she'll find the exit doors, and when the bus arrives she'll guide me up the steps...'

Puzzled, Casey said, 'That's what she's been trained to do.'

'Until yesterday I'd been fighting this whole process,' Bryden said with subdued violence. 'Fighting Bess—and indirectly, you, I suppose. But do you know what I'm beginning to realise, Casey? I can go anywhere with her. Into shops and on buses and across city streets...I don't have to walk slowly with a white cane held out in front of me, and ask for help at every turn.'

Intent on their own business, supremely incurious, the shoppers and businessmen eddied around Casey and Bryden, granting them as much privacy as if they had been standing alone in a field. Casey said fairly, 'Sometimes you'll have to ask for help. And you always have to know where you're going.'

'Just think of what I'm gaining, though. Freedom, Casey. Independence.' His voice changed. 'Give me your hand.'

Even if David Canning had been standing right beside her, Casey could not have refused. Bryden took her fingers and squeezed them between his own; the contact seared every nerve in her body. 'I have you to thank,' he said. 'I know how hard you've worked the last two weeks—you put everything you've got into your job, don't you?'

His intensity had brought tears to her eyes. Trying to be flip, she gulped, 'So does Bess.'

His smile was twisted. 'I promise that in a minute I will pat Bess and tell her she's the most wonderful dog in the world. But right now it's your turn.' He leaned forward and kissed her on the cheek; and, when he did so, felt the wetness of her tears. He said fiercely, 'I didn't mean to make you cry... don't cry, please.'

She spoke a small part of the truth. 'I've been afraid for you and Bess. Afraid you weren't going to make it.'

'You don't need to be. Not any more.' His lips brushed her cheek again. 'Thank you, Casey.'

The floor of the mall rocked and settled. 'You're welcome,' Casey mumbled.

When Bryden stooped to praise Bess, just as if nothing had happened, Casey had to thrust her hands into her pockets so she would not lace her fingers in his thick dark hair. It was just as well that Douglas was nowhere in sight. Her scarlet face would be no advertisement for a cool, detached instructor.

'Shall we go?' Bryden suggested, his smile crackling with vitality. 'Forward, Bess.'

The trip on the bus was accomplished without incident, and Douglas was already waiting for them in the van. Perhaps inwardly Casey had worried that Bryden might repeat his gesture in some way, and thereby cause her embarrassment. She need not have worried. He did not then, nor did he as the April days passed one by one. Instead he worked with a ferocious concentration that she could only applaud, as if determined to learn everything he could; and day by day the bond between him and the golden-haired dog grew stronger.

Some kind of barrier deep within him had fallen, Casey knew; and acknowledged with a rather desperate attempt at humour that she had never thought to find herself jealous of a dog. At a much deeper level of her psyche she was beginning to acknowledge something else: the nightmare prospect that Bryden, at the end of the course, would disappear from her life as thoroughly as he had eight months ago.

She took what comfort she could from the fact that both David Canning and Douglas were well pleased with her work and had certainly observed nothing untoward between her and Bryden. What, after all, had there been to observe? A brief clash in the paddock, when she had told Bryden he meant nothing to her. A couple of kisses that had by no means been impassioned and that she now construed as gratitude.

It did not seem much for nineteen days.

On the last weekend of the course it was Casey's custom to take her students to her parents' home for Sunday afternoon tea, where the warm welcome Bill and Marion Landrigan always extended helped to dispel the homesickness that had often accumulated by the final few days. This time Casey was careful to offer the invitation when both Carole and Bryden were there. However, Carole had other plans, that included Hartley. One romance at the school was flourishing, thought Casey, hesitating a fraction too long before saying, 'Bryden? Will you come?'

His face had that shuttered look that she so dreaded. 'Thank you, I'd like to,' he said in a precise voice that masked any trace of feeling.

'We'll leave around one-thirty,' she said quickly, and fled from the room, not sure whether to be appalled or ecstatic at the prospect of an afternoon in his company. But when the time came she found herself dressing with unusual care in a full skirt of forest-green, an off-white mohair sweater and gleaming leather boots, her hair in a thick braid, her make-up impeccable. The final touch was a fringed green scarf flung artistically over one shoulder. Unfortunately she could do nothing about the state of her nerves.

Bryden was waiting for her outside the school. She drew up beside him, wondering with a sickening lurch of her heart what she was going to talk about all the way to her parents'. It was a forty-minute drive. She had to say something. Her mind a blank, she reached over to open the door.

Bryden solved the problem for her. Once he was settled, with Bess at his feet, he said, 'I don't know why you're doing this.'

He had not bothered with any more conventional greeting. Casey drove on to the highway, heading south. 'Because my parents invited you for tea,' she said.

'As they invite all your students.'

'That's right.'

'Nothing special about me,' he persisted.

'You didn't have to come! But now that you're committed, I hope you'll at least be polite.'

'Oh, my manners are excellent,' he replied ironically.

They then drove in silence for twenty minutes, a silence that seemed to beat against Casey's ears. Bryden was the one to break it. 'Where are we?' he asked.

'On a country road east of the school.'

'Would you mind pulling over for a minute?'

She glanced at him, caught by something in his tone. 'Are you all right?'

'Pull over, Casey.'

She did so; this was a back road and there was little traffic. As the car came to a stop, Bryden reached over, turned off the ignition and pocketed the key. She gave a squawk of indignation. 'What are you doing?'

He favoured her with the smile that had always had the power to weaken her knees and said, 'Is Douglas following in a ten-ton tank with all the guns trained on us?'

'He is not.'

'Is Mr Canning peering at us through the shrubbery?'

'Mr Canning spends every Sunday in the bosom of his family,' Casey replied. 'Bryden, what are you up to?'

'You still wear the same perfume,' he said.

Although she had not really expected he would remember, she had chosen the perfume on purpose. Wondering if she had been altogether wise, she said severely, 'Give me the key.'

'When I'm ready,' he replied with another lazy smile. 'There's something I want to find out first.'

Reprehensibly, part of her was enjoying this. 'We'll be late for tea,' she said.

'I'll leave you to explain why.' Then he put his arms around her in a comprehensive hug, tilted her chin with one hand and kissed her with great thoroughness and very little regard for her lipstick. His quickened breathing fanning her cheek, he said, 'I've been wanting to do that for three weeks.' Releasing her, he sat back, looking undeniably pleased with himself.

Feeling as though the whole world had tilted on its axis, Casey said faintly, 'You've got lipstick on your chin.'

'Unless you want your mother to know you've been misbehaving with a student—and on the Sabbath, no less—you'd better wipe it off.'

She undid her shoulder-bag and extract a Kleenex, with which she scrubbed at his mouth. 'You shouldn't have kissed me,' she muttered, secretly admiring the sculpted line of his upper lip.

'I wanted to find out if you're as indifferent to me as you keep saying you are.' He extracted the key from his pocket and held it out to her, his teeth gleaming as he smiled at her. 'Shouldn't we go? I wouldn't want to disappoint your parents.'

Casey jammed the key in the ignition and checked the rear-view mirror, seeing the bright-eyed reflection and overly pink cheeks of a woman who had been far from indifferent. 'My father has eyes in the back of his head,' she said despairingly, pulling out into the road.

'I promise I shall not ravish your lily-white body on the hall carpet.'

Struck dumb, Casey glared at the highway, her hands gripping the wheel as if she were steering a very small boat in a very rough sea, and conspicously said nothing.

'Would you like me to?' Bryden asked.

'That's a ridiculous and totally unfair question!'

'Because it might jeopardise your job?'

'Nothing to do with my job,' she fumed.

'Good.'

'All right then,' Casey suddenly snorted. 'Now it's my turn to ask a question. Do you still think I deliberately lied to you last September, Bryden? That I went to the cottage knowing you were blind and set out to get your attention? Because if you do, I'm not particularly flattered by any suggestions you make concerning the hall carpet!'

For a long moment he was silent. She stole a glance at his profile, remembering with a wrench at her heart-strings the stark granite cliffs that edged the beach. Finally he said, 'No. I think Jenny was behind it. But not you.'

Discovering she was still furiously angry, Casey snapped, 'When did you come to the conclusion that I'd been telling the truth?'

'Oh, the day after you left the cottage,' he said bitterly.

She remembered all the times she had hoped for a phone call or a letter, and with answering bitterness cried, 'Why did you never *tell* me that?'

'I couldn't at the time—I wasn't ready. Later, of course, I wasn't sure it would matter to you.'

'You called me a liar, and now you say it wouldn't matter to me?'

'Casey, you told me in the paddock that I was no more to you than Hartley. I believed you. Was I then supposed to burst into an impassioned apology for something that happened last autumn?'

She did not want to talk about the paddock. Breathing hard, she said, 'I still don't understand why you didn't tell me last September. Did I mean so little to you that you couldn't even be bothered?'

In a low voice he said, 'You meant far too much to me . . . I couldn't handle it.'

Meant, he had said. Past tense. She slowed down to turn left to the village where her parents lived and said flatly, 'We're nearly there.'

Bryden ignored her. 'I was furious that night when I found out how you earned your living. Because it meant that all week you hadn't been interested in me for myself—I was just an extension of your job.'

'I seem to remember that line,' Casey said, and heard the hurt underlying her words.

'So the next logical step was that you'd set me up. It took me well over twenty-four hours to cool down and realise that the Casey I knew would not have lied to me. By which time you were gone.'

'You knew where I was!'

'I wasn't ready to get in touch with you, Casey! I don't expect you to understand that . . . I'm not sure I understood it myself.'

'I told you more than once that your blindness is ir-relevant,' she said, so quietly that he had to strain to hear her over the sound of the engine.

'I remembered that, too,' he said harshly.

'I *don't* understand.'

He took a deep breath. 'Casey, I'm sorry if I caused you pain.'

It was something; but it was not enough. Not knowing what to say, Casey kept silent.

Bryden's face was bleak; he was absently rubbing Bess's head. 'When I arrived here, I felt as though you'd changed completely. You were the instructor and I was the student—you made that very clear. Serves me right, I guess, after six months of silence.' He gave her a forced and rueful smile. 'Now that the course is nearly over I understand the need for those roles, and I certainly don't want to jeopardise your job in any way, that would be totally wrong of me.' Briefly he rested his hand on hers. 'We're not stuck with them forever.'

As Casey well knew, it was the policy of the school to provide continued supervision and support after the course. 'We're stuck with those roles for at least eight years,' she said wildly. 'I go back to Ragged Island with you next week. In three months I visit you again, and then every year until Bess retires.'

'I swear on a stack of Bibles this discussion will resume before eight years are up,' Bryden said grimly.

Wishing her job had never been invented, Casey said with an air of fatality, 'The driveway's just around the corner.'

'Then slow down. Because there's one more thing I want to say to you.'

The driveway was a long curve between tall trees. Casey stopped beneath the bare branches of the old maple she used to climb as a child; she could see the blue wood-smoke rising from the chimney of the ranch-style bungalow her parents had lived in for thirty years.

Bryden's fist was banging repetitively on his knee, the knuckles white with strain. 'You say my blindness is irrelevant. I want you to think that over very carefully, Casey. Because, apart from any of the other implications, when you make love for the first time you might want to do so with a man who can at least see you.'

She put her foot on the accelerator, and the other trees, mountain ash and birch, began to slide past the car windows. She said without finesse, 'When I make love for the first time, Bryden, I want to do so with the man whom I love more than anyone else in the world. Any other considerations are, if you'll pardon my using the word again, irrelevant...ah, there's my mother. I bet she's checking to see how many of the bulbs survived the winter.' Winding down the window, Casey called, 'Hi, Mum!'

She jumped out of the car and hugged her mother, then led her round to meet Bryden. He was wearing his red ski-jacket and a lambswool sweater the same colour as his eyes, and looked, she thought, quite devastatingly handsome. Which did not mean he was the man she loved more than anyone else in the world. Did it?

Her manner a little over-animated, she made the introductions and explained Carole's absence. Her mother led Bryden over to admire the early crocuses; she had the gift of putting strangers immediately at ease. She looked wonderful, Casey thought affectionately, slim and vibrant, her cap of pewter-coloured hair shining in the sun. Then Casey's father, Bill Landrigan, joined them, his bluff welcome just as sincere. He insisted on taking Bryden on a tour of his beloved greenhouse, where he raised orchids and was attempting to create new strains of primroses and irises. 'I had thirty-five years in the classroom,' he said to Bryden, guiding his hand to the iridescent pink petals of a moth orchid. 'Isn't she a beauty? A grand total of one thousand, one hundred and forty-three eight-year-olds. Not to mention school-boards and unions, which generally were far more trouble than the children. Do you wonder that I enjoy the peace and quiet of my greenhouse?'

'It smells like a tropical rain forest,' Bryden commented.

It was exactly the right reply. Bill approved of Bryden, Casey could see. 'I've installed a very complicated system of pumps—my next project is a fountain. *Ascocenda* loves running water.'

'And they all love the dirt floor,' Marion said with fastidious distaste.

Bill grinned. 'Bryden, the closest Marion and I have ever come to a divorce was when she decided to house-clean here one day—threw out all the seeds from my first-generation crosses of *Primula beesiana* and *Primula bulleyana.*'

'All I did was dust the counter,' Marion protested.

Bill gave his wife a hug. 'I must love you, my darling, if we survived that. The parts for the fountain should arrive on Tuesday, Casey.'

Casey had been watching Bryden. There were frown lines between his eyes, which she was almost certain were a reaction to her father's casually spoken words of love. She said lightly, 'You'll be serving dinner in here that night, Mum.'

'I won't be serving dinner at all—it's a class night,' her mother replied with rather touching pride.

'Mum's started a degree in philosophy at Carleton University,' Casey explained. Carleton was in Ottawa.

Marion said a little defensively, for this was a new venture for her, 'One day, after Bill had counted the number of students he'd had, *I* added up how many apple pies I'd made in the last thirty years. So I decided it was time for a change.'

'Plato would tend to put apple pies in their proper perspective,' Bryden said drily. 'Have you ever, for instance, baked the Ideal Apple Pie?'

Marion laughed, tucking his arm in hers. 'I have not. However, this morning I did make a chocolate cake that approaches perfection.' She smiled up at him, and, a little reluctantly, he smiled as well.

Casey, unaware that her heart was in her eyes, watched them leave the greenhouse. Bill said gruffly, 'I always knew sooner or later you'd fall in love.'

She gaped at him. 'I haven't!'

'I suppose you're worrying because you've only known him three weeks. I was in love with your mother five minutes after I met her.'

'I met Bryden once before,' Casey confessed, gazing absorbedly at the tawny petals of a slipper orchid. 'Last September when I was on holiday in Nova Scotia.'

'You didn't tell us.'

'He kicked me out.'

Her father laughed heartlessly. 'Good for him. You've always been able to wrap all your dates around your little finger, I'm glad to hear he's different.'

He was different in more ways than that. But there were limits to what she could share with her father. 'He's a loner who's scared of his own emotions,' she said.

Bill's gaze was both shrewd and kind. 'I would suspect that he has them, though. Come on, I'll pour you a sherry.'

Shortly afterwards Casey's sister Anne arrived complete with husband and two children. Anne wanted to go for a walk along the trail behind the house to look for wild violets, so eventually they all set off, Bryden letting Bess run free as he fell into conversation with Casey's father. Anne said softly, 'That has to be the best-looking man I've seen off a movie screen. And Dad likes him, you can tell.'

Casey had to agree with both these statements. Anne added provocatively, 'You like him, too.'

Anne, nine years older than Casey, blonde-haired and rather plump, was happily married and wanted the same fate for Casey. 'He's a student,' Casey said repressively.

'If the children weren't in earshot I'd say something very rude. Has he fallen in love with you yet?'

'No—and he has no intention of doing so!'

'Interesting...I'm going to test him out,' Anne said, and fell back before Casey could protest.

Casey's niece Leeanne seized her hand. 'Where are the violets, I can't find any, d'you think we're too early?'

The violets were located, tiny purple faces among the dead beech leaves, and Bess was restrained from tramping on them. Tea was served when they got back to the house; Casey's father and Anne's husband Jim got into their usual political discussion, one in which Bryden more than held his own, and the children got chocolate cake all over their faces. A normal Sunday afternoon, thought Casey, then knew she was guilty of self-deception. How could it be normal when Bryden was there?

She frowned, hoping he was enjoying himself. His manners were indeed excellent, and he was by no means standing on the sidelines; yet she, who knew him well, was certain he was holding something back. He was not truly a part of the gathering, for all his seeming participation. He was...she sought for the right word. Watchful.

Anne whispered in her ear, 'You can't take your eyes off the man.'

Casey pulled a face and went to start on the dishes. Anne and Jim left. Casey finished cleaning up the kitchen, then said without enthusiasm, 'We should get back, Bryden.'

He stood up and in his deep voice said to Bill and Marion, 'Having met Casey's parents, I understand more clearly her qualities of honesty, warmth and kindness...thank you both for your hospitality.'

Marion gave him a spontaneous hug, Bill shook his hand, and Casey blushed. Avoiding her father's eyes, she kissed both her parents and got out of the house as quickly as she could. As she started down the road, Bess fell asleep at Bryden's feet and Bryden seemed disinclined to talk, so she concentrated on her driving and tried not to think about the man at her side.

She managed this for maybe five minutes. Then she stole a glance at him, wondering what he was thinking about. His eyes were closed, his chin set. She blurted, 'Didn't you like my father and mother, Bryden?'

'They're wonderful people—you're very fortunate.'

He had bitten off the words as if they hurt. She ventured, 'You haven't told me much about your parents.'

'One reason I left Ottawa was because my mother was weeping and howling all over me, while my father thought I was making far too much fuss over a minor inconvenience like blindness.'

Casey digested this in silence. 'I know I'm fortunate—I grew up surrounded by love. Taking it for granted, perhaps.'

'Don't. It's rarer than you think.'

He leaned his head against the back of the seat. No more revelations about his parents, she thought, absently counting the crows flying across a field of winter rye, and giving an unconsciously heavy sigh. Seven crows a secret. Bryden was full of those...

Almost as though she had spoken aloud, Bryden said, 'Your sister Anne got a great deal of information out of me—I'm not quite sure how. She's afraid you'll marry Douglas. Douglas, according to her, is nice, but dull.'

'She thinks you're better-looking,' Casey rejoined with a lightness she did not feel.

He raised one brow. 'She extended an open invitation for me to visit her and Jim.'

'She's been throwing me at various men since I was eighteen, Bryden.'

'But none of them took. I wonder why.'

'That will give you something to think about when you get back to the school,' Casey said waspishly.

'So it will . . . I didn't tell Anne everything, though.'

After a brief struggle Casey's curiosity got the better of her. 'What didn't you tell her?'

'She was extolling your virtues, among which honesty figured large. I didn't tell her that I thought you'd been dishonest with me at least once, Casey—that day in the paddock.'

His voice was casual. But the skin was tight across his knuckles, and she sensed that her reply was of over-whelming importance to him. With startling clarity she suddenly knew she wanted this man, wanted him in ways she had never wanted a man before. Ways perhaps beyond her imagining. The ways of intimacy, she thought soberly. She did not understand his defensiveness and his silences any more than she understood his fear of emotion; yet surely the very least gift she could give him was that of honesty?

She said calmly, 'I wasn't telling the truth that day— I suppose I was trying to protect myself.'

Something in his face relaxed. 'So I'm more to you than Hartley, and I'm not just half a unit.'

Her words must have rankled. 'Right,' she said drily.

Stretching his long limbs, he drawled, 'I think it would now be advisable for us to go back to our roles as student and instructor. In the interests of professional ethics.'

Casey had wanted him to pursue that conversation in the paddock, to precipitate her into admitting the way she felt about him. Her emotions in a turmoil, she said nastily, 'Only eight more years, Bryden,' and snapped her mouth shut.

CHAPTER EIGHT

THE last four days of the course flew by. Because of the constraints of geography, it had been decided Casey would fly to Halifax with Bryden on Friday, spend a couple of days with him, and then drive to Marsha's home in New Brunswick; Douglas would look after Hartley and Carole, who lived within a hundred miles of each other on the west coast.

There was the usual Thursday evening party, which came to an end around nine-thirty. Douglas and Casey left the school together, walking across the pavement in the cool, starlit darkness to Casey's car. As she threw her bag on the back seat, Douglas said, 'I was discussing your appraisal today with David—we're both very pleased with your participation in this course, Casey. I'm particularly pleased about the way you've worked with Bryden—there was some concern about that at the beginning of the class, if you remember.'

She could scarcely have forgotten. 'That's good,' she said lightly. 'I'm wiped, though, are you?'

Douglas ignored this undoubted red herring and ploughed on. 'Any worries I might have had on my own account have certainly been allayed. I can see there's nothing of a personal nature between you and Bryden.'

Casey stared at him in silence. It was not the moment to realise, with absolute certainty, that she was in love with Bryden. Had been, probably, since the first time she had seen him, stretched out half naked on the grass. Trying to subdue the mingling of terror and exaltation that this knowledge aroused in her, wishing Douglas were a million miles away, she stammered, 'I-I've got to go home, Douglas, I haven't packed yet and yesterday's dishes are still in the sink.'

Douglas, normally the most sensitive of men, was frowning to himself. 'I will admit I'd rather I was travelling with Bryden tomorrow—no aspersions on you, of course, Casey,' he added hastily. 'I have total trust in you.'

Which was more than she had in herself. Guilt now adding itself to all her other emotions, she edged the car door open and said with a sprightliness that grated on her nerves. 'You just don't want to chaperone Carole and Hartley.'

'Nice to see them happy together,' Douglas said with a meaningful look. 'By the way, David and I were also discussing some future scheduling today. Looks as if I'll be doing interviews in Nova Scotia in July, so I can look after the three-month visit with Bryden.'

He was smiling at her indulgently, and obviously expected her to be delighted with this decision. Casey fought down a wave of fury, said crisply, 'As his instructor I would have thought I'd have been included in that decision, Douglas,' and got in the car. 'See you in the morning. Goodnight.'

She backed out, leaving him standing with a perplexed frown on his face, and drove home; and all her emotions drove home with her. Not until she was unlocking the door of her apartment did she acknowledge that she should have waited a week to discover she was in love with Bryden: her timing was atrocious. For the next two days her role was to be his instructor and the official representative of the school. For some reason it seemed more important to preserve this role when she would be a thousand miles from the school than when she was right under David Canning's nose.

She must, therefore, maintain a dignified distance between herself and Bryden and not even let the word love into her mind.

How? whispered a little voice in her ear.

I don't know, she admitted in despair, and began to wash the dishes.

Casey was very much on her dignity when she loaded Bryden's suitcase in her car the next morning. She was wearing her green skirt, the fringed scarf now elegantly draped in the neckline of a brown leather jacket. Her make-up was generous, in an effort to hide the fact that she had had almost no sleep the night before, and her manner was as impersonal as Douglas could have wished.

Bryden, in a grey suit and navy overcoat, looked both sophisticated and handsome, and appeared not to notice any change in her. Bess was groomed to perfection.

They drove to the airport, making only desultory conversation, walked from the car park to the terminal, and crossed the floor to the ticket counters. They attracted quite a lot of attention, Casey noticed. Bryden was the kind of man who would always draw a second glance, particularly from the female half of the population, while the sleek golden dog at his left side evoked everything from interest to outright sentimentality. That she, on his other side, looked composed and beautiful would have surprised her; make-up, she would have thought, could accomplish only so much, and the prospect of flying, as always, terrified her.

Their seats were in the first-class section against the bulkhead so there would be room for Bess. 'Why don't you take the window-seat?' Bryden suggested.

'No, thanks,' Casey answered hastily. Watching the ground tilt and the clouds envelop her made her feel worse, not better.

The stewardess, who was obviously smitten with Bryden, offered them drinks. Casey shook her head, for she had learned long ago that alcohol did nothing to settle her nerves when she was thirty thousand feet above the ground; Bryden was served a Scotch and water.

The other passengers filtered on. The door was closed. The plane taxied away from the terminal, and while it was awaiting clearance from the tower the stewardess went through the safety regulations. Casey hated this routine almost as much as she hated take-off, for phrases like 'should an incident occur in flight' had always seemed to her the ultimate in euphemism.

They manoeuvred on to the runway, the engines roared into full power and the plane surged forward. Casey closed her eyes and gripped the armrests.

Bryden said casually, 'What is it, a two-hour flight to Halifax, Casey?'

But Casey was concentrating on willing the plane up into the air, and did not answer. He turned his head, touched her lightly on the wrist, and felt the tendons as taut as if she were physically trying to lift the plane herself. 'Casey?' he said sharply. 'What's wrong?'

In a muffled voice she said, 'I'm a little frightened of flying. Ignore me.'

The wheels were no longer bouncing on the tarmac. Tilted at an angle, the aircraft rose into the sky. With some difficulty Bryden detached Casey's left hand from the armrest and chafed it within his own. 'A little frightened?' he said sceptically. 'Wouldn't terrified be more accurate? You should have told me.'

'No point.' She winced as the undercarriage was retracted, her fingers convulsively clutching his.

She was very grateful that he made no attempt to rationalise her fears away; instead he said comfortingly, 'It's lousy when you're really afraid of something, isn't it? Particularly when the rest of the world takes it in its stride.'

'I fly quite often—I have to, because of my job,' she said in a staccato voice. 'I've never told Douglas.'

'Once we level off and the seat-belt sign goes off, you can put your head on my shoulder and go to sleep.'

'But *I'm* supposed to be looking after *you*!' And preserving my dignity, she thought helplessly.

'Look on it this way,' Bryden replied, laughter warming his voice. 'You're giving me the chance to prove what a big strong man I am.'

For a moment her fear receded. She said spontaneously, 'Bryden, I really like you.'

'I like you, too,' he replied, and fumbled for the latch on the armrest.

Fortunately the seats across the aisle were unoccupied. Casey rested her cheek chastely on Bryden's broad shoulder and closed her eyes. She would recapture her dignity once they were on the ground again, and she would hold on to it firmly for the next forty-eight hours.

The engines had settled into a dull drone, and Casey was extremely tired. Her head drooped and her breathing deepened.

The officious voice of the stewardess wakened her. 'The armrest must go up for landing, madam.'

'Why are we landing so soon?' Casey gasped. 'What's wrong?'

Bryden said easily, 'We're coming into Halifax.'

She sat up. His arm was around her, and she had the fleeting remembrance of his heartbeat against her cheek.

'I wish she hadn't woken me up,' she gulped. 'Because I hate landing worse than taking off.'

He gave her shoulders a quick squeeze. 'I have a favour to ask you—do you mind if we drive into the city and do a couple of routes with Bess in the business section and around the university before we head to Ragged Island? I go to Halifax once a month at least…if you've got a piece of paper I can describe the areas I'd need to know.'

As he began listing streets and office complexes her pencil flew over the page, although her ears stayed alert for the lowering of the flaps. 'We could pick up a map at the car rental,' she suggested, then gave a yelp of alarm as the wheels hit the runway. The flaps screamed. The plane slowed down, and gradually her pulse did the same. 'I've dropped the pencil,' she confessed.

'It accomplished its purpose,' Bryden said wryly. 'What's the weather like here?'

She peered through the window. 'Patches of dirty snow and a bad-tempered sky.'

The sky more than lived up to its description as Casey, Bryden and Bess walked the downtown streets of Halifax. The wind from the harbour, tunnelled between the tall buildings, threw grit in their eyes and penetrated every chink in their clothing; the snow in the gutters was more black than white, while the pedestrians looked pale and hunched and out of sorts. 'This is the season they call spring,' Bryden grunted. 'If you can just find the Xerox Building we'll call it quits and head uptown.'

The university area was more pleasant to look at, but no less cold. After they left there, they went to a grocery shop in one of the malls and stocked up on food for Bryden and for Bess; then Casey battled the late afternoon traffic out of the city.

It was almost dark when they turned into Bryden's driveway, the house a stark black outline among the trees. 'Well, Bess,' Bryden said softly, 'this is your new home.'

Bess, predictably, wagged her tail. Casey said, 'Be careful when you get out, Bryden, there are patches of ice between here and the house. Shall I unlock the door?'

He passed her the key. 'I'll let Bess have a run in the garden.'

The house was cold, and Casey's footsteps made the floorboards creak. She flicked on some lights, turned up the furnace and went back to get the groceries. If she had any sense she would leave right away for the bed and breakfast where she had a reservation. But there was no family to welcome Bryden home, no hot meal ready for him, no fire blazing in the hearth; she did not want him to be alone on his first evening home. Anyway, she thought with a toss of her head, she was hungry and restaurants were few and far between along the shore at this time of year. She had been lucky to find a place to stay.

While Bess sniffed in all the corners, Bryden helped Casey with the luggage and the groceries. Then he said, 'I bought two fillets, Casey... you'll stay for dinner?'

'I'd love to,' she said.

He was standing by the counter in the kitchen, a lettuce in one hand and a bag of tomatoes in the other; he gave her a smile that melted her heart and said huskily, 'There were lots of nights last winter when I never thought you'd be here again.'

'There were lots of nights when I never thought I would be, either.'

'I was a fool not to get in touch with you—I'm sorry.'

'You're forgiven,' she said, and discovered it was true. Then belatedly she remembered she was on duty, that this evening was as much a part of her job as the supervised lessons at the school, and added with a touch of severity, 'Do you want me to make the salad?'

'It's OK, Casey, I'm not going to jump on you,' Bryden said shortly. 'But we can be friendly, can't we?'

Only five minutes ago she had carried his suitcase up to his bedroom, whose tall windows overlooked the ocean. He had a king-size bed heaped with silk cushions that glowed like jewels, and she had been stabbed by a desire so sharp as to cause her pain. Friendly, he had said. 'I guess so,' she replied.

'All right, then. Why don't you pour each of us a drink? I keep the alcohol in the corner cupboard in the living-room.'

She had survived the plane trip, and she would be gone from here right after supper. She mixed a Scotch and water for Bryden and a rum and coke for herself, passed him his glass and clinked hers with his. She said seriously, 'To you and Bess, Bryden—a good partnership.'

He said just as seriously, 'You made it so, Casey. I learned such a lot about you the last month...you never once lost your patience, and your encouragement of me. was steadfast, rock-solid, never faltering even on the worst of days—because you believe in what you do.' He took a long pull at his drink. 'You were always there when you were needed, yet in four weeks Bess and I have become an independent unit. That takes skill. Skill and caring.'

Although Casey had been praised for her work before, she knew she would cherish Bryden's words to the end of her days. 'Thank you,' she said, and cleared her throat. 'You worked hard, too. So did Bess.'

He was standing on the far side of the counter, gripping its edge. 'You're changing my life...you know that, don't you?'

Suddenly panic-stricken—for what if he only meant that she was increasing his ability to deal with his blindness by making him more independent?—Casey said flippantly, 'You could change my life right now by cooking me dinner—I'm starving.'

'I've never thought you were a coward, Casey.'

Nor had she. But then she had never been in love before. She said with frantic truth, 'I don't think we should have any conversations we wouldn't want Douglas to hear.'

Bryden said pithily, 'To hell with Douglas.'

'I *am* on duty, Bryden,' Casey replied, and winced at her own pomposity.

'Thanks for reminding me.'

He had unquestionably snarled at her. 'I don't have to stay for supper,' she said haughtily.

'Dammit, Casey, will you stop acting as if Douglas were sitting on your shoulder?'

'Why don't *you* stop yelling?'

'You're the first woman I've ever yelled at in my life!'

'Is that supposed to be a compliment?'

'I think perhaps it is,' Bryden said with undoubted menace. 'Because with any of the other women you wouldn't see me for dust if I thought my emotions were in danger of getting involved. I'd run. Run as fast as I knew how. But I don't want to run away from you, Casey. I want to shake you until your teeth rattle. I want to kiss you until you melt in my arms. I want to haul you up to bed. But run—no, thanks.'

Trying to ignore the last part of this all-inclusive speech, Casey said spiritedly, 'And just how many other women were there, Bryden?'

'Jealous, Casey?'

Horribly. 'I would be being dishonest if I were to say no,' she answered, a quiver of laughter in her voice.

'I find your rare urges to dishonesty as interesting as your rectitude,' Bryden said, tossing back his drink. 'Unfortunately the word rectitude reminds me of the shade of Douglas. I shall feed the dog if you would care to start the salad, Casey.'

'You're not the only one whose teeth could do with rattling,' she said breathlessly. 'Vinaigrette or mayonnaise?'

'Your choice.' He gave her a grin that drove every recipe she knew out of her head. 'I discover in myself a person I never thought existed when I'm with you.'

She said slowly, 'I felt that way about myself when I met you last September.'

'Sooner or later we're going to have to give Douglas—and the director—the boot, Casey.'

Again she felt that flicker of panic. 'We can't when I'm here on business.'

'If I can deal with elliptic equations I should be able to work around that. Now, Bess, where did I put your food?'

'In the cupboard to the right of the sink,' said Casey, and tried to focus her brain on the ingredients for salad dressing.

Between them, and perhaps to the surprise of each, they produced a delicious meal, which they ate by candle-light at the pine table in the kitchen alcove. Bryden, who seemed to have forgotten his outburst, was a charming host, while Casey sparkled in conversation; and not one of the topics they covered would have caused Douglas disquiet. Afterwards they cleaned up the kitchen. Then Casey said with a regretful sigh, 'Bryden, I've got to go—I'm dead on my feet. I'll be back around nine-thirty tomorrow morning.'

He said gently, 'The other thing I learned about you the past month is how hard you work—you must be tired. Be careful on the ice outside, won't you? And sleep well, Casey.' He made no attempt to touch her as he held the door open.

Casey had wondered if she might have to drag in professional ethics again; obviously not. 'Goodnight,' she said, went down the steps and crossed the driveway to the rented car, absently noticing that the ice was the worst between the high cedar hedges where the sun could not penetrate. Tomorrow she must spread some sand there.

When she started the car its tyres whined as they sought traction, then the vehicle jerked dramatically as the wheels dug into the dirt. She backed out of the driveway and turned towards the village.

She had made her reservation at Ragged Harbour's only bed and breakfast two weeks ago, and had said she would probably be late checking in. As she approached the village the lights twinkled cheerfully through the trees, and she kept her eye out for the signpost: at the far end of the village, the owner, a Miss Elvira Worthington, had said. Casey pictured her as tall and rather forbidding, her furniture and moral standards as being of the Victorian era.

The sign was attractive, hand-carved and gilded; the house had gables and rigidly pruned yew bushes. It was also, Casey noticed with faint unease, in darkness apart from a light over the front door. She parked the car, ran up the brick path to the door and pressed the bell. It jangled inside.

The house remained in darkness. No Miss Elvira Worthington to chide her for lateness; no sounds at all. Casey pressed the bell again, and for good measure banged the ornate, cast-iron knocker.

A car slowed up on the highway. A man's voice called, 'You lookin' for Elvira?' Casey nodded vigorously, walking across the cropped grass towards the road. 'She's in hospital,' the man said; although bearded like Simon, he was as talkative as Simon was silent. 'Took a turn last Tuesday. Today's the first day she's been herself at all. C'n I help?'

'I've got a reservation to stay the night,' Casey said unhappily.

'Well, now...' The man frowned prodigiously. 'You might try the Havestock Motel in Martin's Cove. Although I'm of the opinion they don't open until late in May. Nothin' else short of Halifax or Millerton.'

Millerton was as far west as Halifax was east. Casey said, 'I'll go to the phone booth and try the motel. Thanks for your help.'

The motel's phone rang unanswered. Casey tried two other motels in the area with the same lack of success, by which time she had run out of quarters. The tourist season was not under way in late April in Nova Scotia; why should it be, when there was still ice in the ditches and snow on the hills? Nevertheless, she drove to the little variety shop at the other end of the village to get some more quarters.

The shop had closed five minutes before she'd got there. She stood outside in the chill, damp air, wondering what to do.

The choices were not many. She could drive to Halifax or Millerton, which would take over an hour; or she could go back to Bryden's. Encased in professional ethics, she thought dourly. And what would she tell David Canning when she could not produce a receipt for her two nights in Ragged Island?

Halifax was the logical destination; it was a big enough city that she would have no trouble finding a place to stay. But even as she reached this conclusion, she felt a dead weight of exhaustion descend on her. She could not face the drive back to the city.

She would go to Bryden's.

CHAPTER NINE

FIVE minutes later Casey was turning into Bryden's driveway again. She parked nearer the road this time, not wanting to skid on the ice, and through the flat cedar fronds saw that he had switched off the outside light. She reached for her overnight bag in the back seat, hoping he had not gone to bed.

Her scarf caught in the door-handle as she shut it; it was a measure of Casey's tiredness that this added mishap brought tears to her eyes. She blinked them back, took off her gloves, freed the fringe of the scarf, which now had grease on it, and picked up her bag again. Trudging down the driveway, she searched the upstairs windows for any signs of life. Bryden, of course, would not need lights. Surely he wouldn't be asleep already?

She was almost at the steps when the leather heel of her boot slipped on a patch of ice and her feet went out from under her. Her bag threw her further off balance; she crashed to the ground, her shoulder striking the edge of the steps, her hand bent under her. Inside the house Bess began barking.

Casey lay very still, temporarily stunned. The door opened. Bryden said loudly, 'Who's there? Steady, Bess, *steady*!'

'It's me,' Casey mumbled, and added with professional accuracy and a slightly hysterical giggle, 'at the bottom of your steps. On your left.'

'*Casey!* Sweetheart, are you all right? Don't move...Bess, down!'

143

Casey was not sure she wanted to move. Sweetheart, he had called her. Sweetheart, she thought muzzily, was a beautiful word.

Bryden hurried down the steps, Bess at his heels, and knelt at her side. As he ran his hands over her body, the dog licked her ear. Bryden said urgently, 'Where does it hurt? Did you fall on the ice? I thought of throwing some salt down, but I didn't bother—I wasn't expecting you back. Casey, say something!'

'Why did you call me sweetheart?' she whispered.

She had taken him aback; for a full five seconds he was silent. 'I did, didn't I?' he said slowly. 'I suppose because you scared me half to death.'

'So you didn't mean it?'

'Casey, this is no time for a discussion on Freudian slips of the tongue,' he said impatiently. 'It doesn't feel as though you've broken anything...can you stand up?' He put his arm around her waist. 'Here, lean on me.'

Through his sweater his arm had the tensile strength of steel. After he had pulled her to her feet, she stumbled up the steps and into the house. Bryden kicked the door shut behind him and guided her towards the chester-field, where he eased her down with exquisite care. 'I have no idea what the medical journals would say, but I'm going to get you a brandy,' he said. 'Stay there.'

Casey could not have done otherwise. Shock was wearing off and pain replacing it. Her shoulder felt as if someone had kindled a fire inside it, while her wrist was being rhythmically stabbed with a pick. She felt very cold. When Bryden returned with the brandy in a tumbler, he had to wrap her fingers round the glass and hold them in place; she was shivering.

The first mouthful made her choke; the second burned a trail down her throat and at least supplied a counterirritant to all her other woes. 'The bed and breakfast was closed,' she sputtered. 'The owner is in hospital.'

'No reason for you to try and join her.'

She took another gulp of brandy. 'I shouldn't have come back here. But I was t-too tired to drive back to Halifax.'

'I'd have been furious with you if you had. For heaven's sake, Casey, all this professional ethics stuff is well and good, but you can carry it too far. You're going to finish that brandy, you're going to have a hot bath, and then you'll sleep in the spare room.' Clipping off his words, he went on, 'If it'll make you feel better, I personally will call Mr Canning and explain that the only accommodation in thirty miles was shut and that just for good measure you almost broke your neck on my back steps.'

Rather pleased that Bryden sounded so angry, Casey said meekly, 'Very well.'

'What, no fight?'

'Fighting takes energy,' she replied with a suppressed giggle; the brandy seemed to have surrounded her in a rose-coloured aura.

Bryden raised his brow. 'I suppose your bag is outside at the bottom of the steps.'

'Oh.' Less than convincingly Casey said, 'I'll get it.'

'You will not. And no more brandy, or I'll be carrying you up the stairs.'

'How romantic,' she said dreamily.

'How unprofessional,' was the dry response. 'Hold Bess, will you, while I go outside?'

Cold air wafted around Casey's ankles from the open door; the brandy did not seem to have extended as far as her ankles. Carefully she put the glass on the mahogany table and patted the dog. When Bryden came back carrying her case she pushed herself upright with her good hand and followed him up the stairs. Then she saw that he was carrying her bag into his bedroom, not the spare room.

In a confused rush of emotion Casey wondered what she should do. Scream for help? Make love to Bryden? Much as she might want to do the latter, the time was not right. She hesitated in the doorway, feeling gauche and unhappy, wishing he had not put her in this position.

Bryden said casually, putting her bag down on the floor, 'You can sleep in here rather than the spare room, Casey—it's warmer and the bed's already made up. I'll take the other room.' Then he must have sensed something in the quality of her silence. He scowled at her. 'I see—you were afraid I was setting you up for the big seduction scene.'

'I didn't know what to think,' she faltered.

Her reply had angered him further. 'You can quit worrying,' he rapped. 'I've already said I'm not going to jump on you...apart from all the other considerations, and there are many, the timing's lousy.' He nodded behind him, still frowning. 'The bathroom's through there. Towels in the closet.' He turned on his heel to leave the room.

Casey burst into tears.

It would have been difficult to say who was the more surprised by her action, she or Bryden. As she sat down hard on the bed and buried her face in her hands, sobbing noisily, Bryden uttered an expletive under his breath, sat down beside her and put an arm around her shoulders.

She flinched. 'That hurts,' she hiccuped. 'I banged my shoulder on your step.'

He shifted his arm to her waist and said strongly, 'Listen to me, Cassandra Elizabeth Landrigan. I'm going to turn on the water, then I'll go downstairs and make some hot cocoa. By the time that's ready, you'll be in bed. You will drink it and go to sleep and tomorrow will be a whole new day.'

She snuggled her cheek into his shoulder, thinking she was making a habit of this. 'It couldn't be a worse day than today,' she sighed. 'I was planning to be so dignified and proper and correct. Casey, the perfect instructor...oh, Bryden, you do feel warm.'

He detached himself from her and stood up. 'I'm only flesh and blood,' he said drily. 'I can be tempted. I'll be back in a few minutes with the cocoa.'

He had forgotten to turn on the bath water. Casey did so herself, poured in a generous amount of bubble bath, and with difficulty, because her wrist was very sore, found her nightdress and housecoat in her bag. Her nightdress would not tempt him. It was made of fleecy cotton, reached to her feet and had ruffles at wrist and throat. Not that she had any intention of tempting him, she told herself hastily, and closed the bathroom door.

The gravel in the driveway had scraped her wrist raw, an ominous red blotch on her shoulder would no doubt turn purple by tomorrow, and her face looked like that of a woman who had just cried copiously.

However, fifteen minutes later when Casey lay down in Bryden's bed with the covers pulled up to her chin she was both feeling and looking much better. The curtains were open, so she could see the light flashing on Ragged Island: a solitary light in a blackness that stretched for thousands of miles...her eyelids drooped shut.

A hand was stroking her cheek. 'I'm not really asleep,' she mumbled.

'How do you feel now?'

'Much better.' Bryden was sitting on the edge of the bed. His eyes looked almost black, depthless like the ocean, his hair was tousled, and she was very conscious of the reality of his body beneath his shirt and trousers. It was a good thing he could not read her thoughts.

'Cocoa,' he said.

'Oh, good,' Casey said brightly, and took one of the steaming mugs from the tray that was balanced on his lap. The cocoa was too hot to drink fast. She racked her brains for something innocuous to say. 'Do you have a bed for Bess?'

'When Douglas was here for the interview, he suggested foam rubber with a removable cover. So I had one made.'

'What a good idea.' It was, she thought, just as well that Douglas could not read her thoughts either.

She swallowed the cocoa as fast as she could, and all the while the restraint in the room thickened, palpable as a blanket. 'I'm sure I'll fall right to sleep now,' she said finally, putting her mug back on the tray.

Bryden took the tray and stood up. 'I'd better go.'

'Thank you, Bryden,' Casey said, and in exasperation decided she sounded like a wind-up toy.

But Bryden did not move. His face a mask, he said deliberately, 'I've adjusted reasonably well to my blindness by now. I no longer contemplate cutting my throat. I don't want to break the chairs that I trip over into smithereens, and my hide's getting a little tougher for dealing with those members of the public who want to help me over streets that I don't want to cross. But right now I'd give my fancy braille computer to be able to see the expression on your face—you have no idea how frustrating it is to be second-guessing all the time! You *sound* so sweet and polite—yes, Bryden, no, Bryden, as if you don't give a damn that you're lying in my bed...but what the hell are you thinking?' As she made a strangled sound, he added in disgust, 'I know—I'm an insensitive boor, and you're exhausted.'

Casey found her voice. 'I'm sounding as sugary as Pollyanna so that I *won't* tell you what I'm thinking!'

'Which is?'

If it had been a hard month for her, it had been more difficult for him; she was not the only one who must be exhausted. She said, taking her courage in her hands, 'Bryden, I hope some day we'll be together in your bed. I'd like that. But even though we both know it can't be now, that doesn't mean I'm not capable of being tempted, too.'

The light on Ragged Island flashed and vanished, flashed and vanished. Bryden said quietly, 'You shake my heart with your honesty, Casey.'

Casey said in a small voice, 'You could kiss me goodnight.'

He put the tray down on the bedside table, sat down beside her and braced his hands on the pillow on either side of her head. Then he bent to find her mouth, touching her only with his lips. His kiss made no physical demands; it had more the nature of a pledge, a secret inner promise not yet ready to be put into words. And when it was over he dropped his face into the curve of her shoulder, resting his weight on her and closing his eyes.

With infinite tenderness Casey wrapped her arms around him and held him to her, her cheek against his hair, and allowed the love that she had suppressed all day to wash over her. Perhaps it would reach him, she thought humbly, and bring him whatever comfort he sought.

His breathing was so deep and slow that she wondered if he had fallen asleep. But eventually he raised his head, pushing himself away from her with his palms flat on the bed. Then with one finger he traced the delicate bones of her face, his own face intent. He said softly, 'I don't need to see your expression now...I don't understand how or why, Casey, but you heal me. Heal wounds I'd never acknowledged were there.' Briefly he laid his cheek against hers again. Then he got up from the bed, picked up the tray and strode out of the room.

As Casey lay back on the pillow she caught the faint fragrance of his aftershave, and, more elusively, the scent of his body. Wrapped in happiness, she closed her eyes and fell asleep.

It was pouring with rain when Casey woke up. Getting out of bed was an act of physical courage, because she was sore in places she had not known existed. Walking to the bathroom was comparable to a marathon. Her shoulder, she saw when she stripped for another hot bath, resembled a very lurid sunset, and bruises like small purple clouds were scattered over the rest of her body.

The bath helped. She dressed in jeans and a blue sweater and descended the stairs with great care. Bryden was in the kitchen. She sniffed the air appreciatively and said, 'A man after my own heart—the coffee's brewed.'

'Have you looked out of the window?'

'It's going to be a long walk to the village,' she said philosophically.

She, Bryden and Bess worked extremely hard that day. They walked to the village and traced routes there that Bryden would be likely to use. They walked home and had lunch. Then they drove to Martin's Cove, the nearest town of any size, where they located the various shops Bryden might need, and tracked from one to the next in the teeming rain. Because Bryden had a phenomenal memory they were able to accomplish a lot; but all three were soaked to the skin when they finished at four-thirty.

They trailed up the steps of Bryden's house. His first concern was to dry Bess, so Casey went upstairs and had her third hot bath. She put on a pale pink tracksuit, her feet bare, her hair loose; when she went downstairs Bess was lying on the rug in front of the fireplace, where Bryden had been brushing her. 'I think she wants you to light the fire,' Casey said.

Bryden straightened, his wet hair still clinging to his scalp. 'I'd planned to take you out for dinner tonight,' he said. 'But it would mean driving into Halifax again.'·

She said sincerely, 'I'd much rather have pizza in front of the fire.'

Bryden's rare smile lit his face. 'So would I.'

'I'll make the pizza if you'll light the fire. I like making pizza—lots of room for creativity.'

He laughed. 'There are only two things I can't eat—squid and maraschino cherries.'

That left Casey with plenty of scope. An hour later she and Bryden were sitting side by side on the chesterfield munching thick wedges of pizza, while Bryden tried to list all the ingredients. Casey felt warm and relaxed and happy; she chattered on about her family and about the qualifying exams she would write early in June. 'I'll be glad when they're over,' she admitted, licking her fingers. 'I've got a lot of studying to do.'

'Have you always liked dogs, Casey?'

She was off again, describing the stray cats and dogs her father was always bringing home. 'Unfailingly, the cats were female and pregnant,' she said with a reminiscent smile as she got up to put another log on the fire.

They had not bothered to switch on any lights; at their backs, through the tall windows, was the black of ocean and sky and the beat of rain, with only the small circle of orange and yellow light at their faces. Casey sat down again. 'Did you ever have another pet, Bryden—after the puppy?'

'No. I was sent off to boarding school soon afterwards.'

At the age of six. Casey swallowed a flash of pure rage. 'Was I the first person you ever told about that?'

'Yes.'

'I'm glad you told me,' she said, adding fiercely, 'Not all fathers are like yours.'

'And I can't live the rest of my life in his shadow...I'm starting to understand that.' He drained the last of the wine from his glass and changed the subject. 'What will you do once exams are over? You're due down here in July.'

She said baldly, 'Douglas will be coming. Not me. He had interviews in this area, so it's the logical thing to happen. I was going to tell you before I left.'

Bryden gave an unamused bark of laughter. 'Douglas doesn't have to worry—you've stuck to your role admirably. Casey the virginal instructor will be returning to the school exactly as she left it.'

'You don't have to be crude!'

'I'm sorry!' he snapped. He got up, picking his way between the furniture to stand facing the window, where the rain trickled down the glass in tiny, intermingling rivers. He said heavily, 'Casey, forget the school. Forget everyone else's expectations. If circumstances were otherwise, would you want to keep on seeing me?'

'I told you I hoped we'd make love.'

'Not just that,' he said roughly. 'More than that.'

'Yes,' she whispered.

If she had then expected to be swept into his arms, she was soon disappointed. Turning to face her, he said violently, 'I hope you know what you're saying.'

'It isn't easy—you tell me very little, Bryden.'

'I know I'm asking a lot of you, Casey. But I've been locked up inside myself for so long...finding you is

forcing me to change in ways that are new for me.' He
raked his fingers through his hair. 'And every minute
I'm with you, I'm fighting to keep my hands off you.'

Trying to make a joke of it, she said, 'We've managed
very well in that respect the last twenty-four hours.'

'We're fools,' he said savagely. 'You'll be leaving tomorrow, and God knows when we'll see each other
again.' He raked his fingers through his hair and added
with an abruptness that was characteristic of him. 'Do
you mind if I go into my study for a while? I need a
break from all this.'

So he needed to be alone. He had spent a great deal
of his life alone, Casey thought, suddenly afraid. Could
she change that? Could anyone? 'Please don't shut me
out, Bryden!' she begged.

He was banging on the window-frame with his fist,
the small repetitive thuds jarring her nerves. He asked,
'What time do you have to leave tomorrow?'

'Eight-thirty at the latest. It's a five-hour drive.'

'I'll be up.' He called Bess and left the room.

She remembered the dreams she had had all winter,
dreams where he had turned his back on her and left her
alone. The rain rattling against the tall windows was now
a threat, and the dying flames brought her no comfort.
She placed the screen in front of the fire and went
upstairs.

The door to the study was closed. She went into
Bryden's room and closed that door as well.

At eight-twenty the next morning Casey was standing
by her car. She and Bryden had eaten breakfast together, making small talk as if they were two strangers,
and then she had loaded her case in the back seat. She
bent and hugged Bess. 'Be a good girl, won't you?' Then
she looked up at Bryden.

His navy blue sweatshirt darkened his eyes. The wind, damp from the sea, played with his hair. 'Bryden?' she said. 'Is this goodbye?'

He clasped her by the sleeves of her leather jacket. 'No,' he said hoarsely. 'I'll see you before summer. I don't know how yet, but I'll work something out...I hate for you to leave, Casey.'

'I'll miss you,' she said helplessly.

His answer was to wrap his arms around her, one hand moulding the line of her spine, the other seeking the fullness of her breast under her jacket. His kiss was another desperate searching. She clung to him, kissing him back with passionate abandon, a surge of desire overwhelming her, blinding her to anything but the present moment.

When he eventually released her, his chest was rising and falling as if he had been running. But all he said was, 'I'll phone you.'

She had wanted a declaration of love, an outpouring of his need for her. She bit her lip, praying she would not cry. 'I'll look forward to that.'

He produced a semblance of a smile. 'We shouldn't have congratulated ourselves last night. One kiss under the cedar hedge and we're in trouble.'

Her heart was still hammering against her ribs from that one kiss. Knowing she could not bear to prolong this scene, Casey whispered, 'Take care of yourself, Bryden.' Then she quickly kissed his cheek, got in the car and backed out of the driveway; the ice had melted in the rain. Her last view was of a tall, blue-eyed man with one hand raised in salute, a golden-haired dog at his side.

She did not know when she would see him again; she did not know if he would ever love her as she craved to be loved. All she knew was that leaving him was the most painful thing she had ever done.

CHAPTER TEN

CASEY put down her pen with a tired sigh. She had written the three essay questions as fully as she could, then she had edited them and checked for spelling mistakes. There was nothing more she could do.

This was her final exam. She looked out of the upstairs window of the office where she had been writing; it was a beautiful day, the oak trees decked in the fresh green of early summer, sun and shade waltzing among the branches.

It was also June, she thought, watching a tiny yellow bird flit through the leaves, and Bryden had promised he would see her before summer. He had phoned her three times, stilted phone calls full of things unsaid that always left Casey on edge and irritable, even while simultaneously she longed for the next one. He had said nothing, for instance, about a visit. And she, intimidated by the distance between them and by the silences that hummed along the line, had been too proud to ask.

Back in April he had sworn it was not goodbye. She had to trust those words, for she really had no other choice. But waiting, she was finding, was very difficult, and her prediction that she would miss him had proved horribly true. She ached for him and longed for him, and she would never again say 'I'll miss you' without realising the inadequacy of the words.

She dragged her thoughts back to the present. In one way she was sorry her exams were over, for they had kept her mind occupied; although this was not something she would tell her parents tonight when she went there for dinner to celebrate the end of the exams. Neatly she arranged the answer booklet inside the question folder and left the office.

David Canning was talking to Brenda, the secretary whose desk was across the hall. He eyed Casey over his glasses. 'How was it?'

'Two or three of the multiple-choice questions had me stymied, but the essay topics were fine.'

'You'll do well, I'm sure.' He smiled at her. 'Going on a pub crawl tonight?'

'Going to have dinner with my parents,' she rejoined with a grin.

'Douglas is away until Friday noon... once he's back I want you to take a couple of days off. Come back next Wednesday, say. You've worked hard the last month, Casey.'

With or without his half-glasses, David Canning missed very little. Casey said ruefully, 'Do I look that bad?'

'You look fine. Together with the weekend, that would give you four days—go away somewhere and forget about the lot of us.'

Her eyes clouded; away meant Ragged Island. Realising the director was still watching her, she smiled determinedly. 'Thanks, David,' she said. 'I'll probably stay home and sleep.'

'You can do better than that,' he said. 'In fact, I'm sure you will.' He picked up some papers from the desk and drifted down the hall. Casey pulled a face which made Brenda giggle, and ran downstairs to her car.

The bungalow looked very peaceful, late daffodils blooming in big clumps like sunbursts among the birches, and the air full of birdsong. Casey parked by the house, tapped on the back door and stepped inside.

Her mother hurried down the steps from the kitchen, wiping her hands on a towel; she looked unusually flustered, as if she had just discovered the head of the philosophy department on her back steps rather than her middle daughter. 'Darling! How did it go today?' She offered her cheek for a kiss. 'Before you get settled, will you do me a favour? Pick a big bunch of pansies for the table from the back borders, would you mind?'

'Have you got the best silver out?' Casey asked in comical dismay. 'I didn't bother going home to change.'

'You look lovely,' Marion said firmly. 'Off you go.'

Casey loved the garden, for her father's untidiness was in full spate in the rampaging perennials and massed bulbs. The pansies were growing wild at the very back, where the garden joined the trees; she knelt and began picking them, charmed as always by their velvet-complexioned faces.

To her right a thrush was singing, its plangent notes cupped in the deep silence of the woods. The fragrance of the flowers in her hand reminded her of the pansies she had picked at the cottage and given to Bryden, so many months ago...

In a loud rustling of last year's leaves, the peace of the garden was disrupted. Casey looked up, startled. A dog was racing through the birches towards her, trampling daffodils as it came. A dog that was as familiar to her as her own face. Bess.

As the dog skidded to a halt, her tail thrashing the air, Casey flung her arms around her. 'Bess, what are you doing here? Yes, it's lovely to see you—but I don't understand!' She pushed Bess away, looking all around her. The thrush was still singing in the woods, and the sun slanting through the birches made silver wands of their trunks. There was no sign of movement. She said slowly, 'Is Bryden here? Bess, is your master here?'

Bess panted sympathetically, and the little bells on her collar jingled. Said Casey, 'Find Bryden, Bess. Find Bryden.'

The dog set off through the daffodils again, purpose in every step. Casey followed, scarcely daring to hope, quite unable to understand. Bryden couldn't be here...here, at her parents' house, on the day she finished exams. Clutching the pansies so hard that their stems were bruised, she threaded her way through the birch trees, and heard in her ears the thudding of her heart.

Bess had come out on the path where last April they had searched for violets, and was trotting along it, looking back over her shoulder to see if Casey was following. Casey was almost running, her turquoise eyes wide open. Although she desperately wanted to believe in this miracle, she was afraid to.

Then she came round a curve in the path, and saw, a hundred feet ahead of her, a man waiting under a tree. A tall man in trousers and a smoke-blue sweater, whose head was turned towards the sound of their approach. Every line of his body was tense.

Bryden.

Casey slowed down, not knowing whether to sing or dance or cry. All her senses heightened, she heard her shoe scrape on a rock, saw the sun glance off the polished surface of a beech leaf, felt the lightest of breezes lift her hair. 'Am I dreaming?' she said softly. 'Am I going to wake up and you'll have vanished? Or are you real, Bryden?'

'Come here, Casey...because I need to know that you're real, as well.'

Like a woman in a trance she closed the distance between them, her eyes seeking out every loved and remembered detail of his appearance. The indigo eyes and broad shoulders were the same, as was the air of holding back, the reserve that he always seemed to carry with him. She said with incredulous joy, 'I can't believe you're here!'

Her voice rang with that joy. Bryden threw his arms around her, almost lifting her off the ground, and kissed her as if his life depended on convincing her she was wanted. She strained into him, kissing him back with generosity and passion, her whole being consumed with a hunger that she could not have hidden from him had she wanted to.

His hands were roaming her body in frantic rediscovery. He breathed against her mouth, 'You're real— my God, you're real! You wouldn't believe how I've waited for this.'

He was dropping quick, hard kisses all over her face. 'Yes, I would,' she said, clasping her hands around his waist and feeling the pounding of his heart against her breast. 'Because I've been waiting, too.'

He kissed her with an explicitness that left her trembling. 'So *this* hasn't changed,' he said.

'Were you afraid it would?'

'When you're not with me, I'm afraid you don't exist,' he said huskily. 'You're the angel on top of the tree, Casey—the miraculous gift I have no right to be given, and very little knowledge of how to receive.'

As always, he had the capacity to reduce her to tears. She whispered, 'That's the most beautiful thing anyone has ever said to me.'

His hug drove the breath from her lungs, and for a long moment they stayed locked in each other's arms. Then Bess whined at their feet, and with a catch of laughter in her voice Casey said, 'The ear that you were kissing Bess kissed first.'

'That tells me where your priorities lie.'

'Furthermore, we're standing in a sea of pansies. Mum sent me out to pick some, and I must have dropped them when you kissed me.' She added in sudden enlightenment, 'Of course, Mum knew you were here—that's why she wouldn't let me in. Have you been in cahoots with my parents, Bryden Moore?'

'Yes,' he said.

'You're not supposed to confess that easily!'

'I've been in Ottawa for the last week, staying with Jenny and Matthew. I had some business to look after and I didn't want to disturb you while you were studying, so when I was talking to your father one day last week he invited me out this evening.'

'That nice little speech is exactly like your phone calls—it doesn't say nearly enough,' Casey announced, and was no longer joking.

With all the force of his personality Bryden replied, 'I know you don't understand. But in two more days I'll have a lot more answers...can you bear with me until then?'

The thrush's song was so far away now that she could scarcely hear it. She said slowly, 'You're shutting me out again, Bryden. Just as you did all last winter.'

'What do you mean?'

For a moment she was silent, for although what she had to say was of crucial importance, it might also drive him away. 'Part of any relationship has to be sharing. It's easy to share the good times—but it's much more difficult to share things like decisions and failures and worries. If you don't, though, the relationship isn't a relationship at all, it's just two separate people. Unconnected. Not real to each other.'

'I've always carried everything alone, Casey.'

'Then you must change,' she said. 'Because it hurts when you shut me out.'

'I don't want to hurt you!'

She clasped his hands in hers, needing their strength and warmth, and said steadily, 'Tell me what answers you might have in two more days, Bryden.'

Because she loved him, she could sense the inner struggle before he spoke. 'I decided last winter I didn't want to go back to my old job, so I applied to Carleton University for a teaching position. They're to phone me Friday morning with the verdict.'

A new job would mean a great deal to him in terms of independence and self-worth. 'Thank you for telling me,' she said quietly. 'I do hope you get it.'

'I'd be based in Ottawa again. Not that far from the school,' he said, and suddenly smiled at her with the vitality that always drove coherent thought from her brain. 'Speaking of which, how did the exams go?'

Knowing that she and Bryden had crossed a major hurdle, Casey bent down and began gathering the pansies, some of which Bess had sat on; she chattered on about the traumas of examinations on whose results depended her three-year apprenticeship while Bryden put Bess's harness back on. By the time they set off for the house the raw emotion of their meeting had receded sufficiently that Casey felt able to face her father's eagle eye.

That evening was one of the happiest of Casey's life, although outwardly nothing out of the ordinary occurred; it was a normal family dinner complete with dissertations on orchids and Aristotle. Yet Casey felt like a child on Christmas morning. She did not have to search far for the reason—he was sitting across from her at the table, laughing at some joke of her father's. Part of the family, she thought, in a way he had not allowed himself to be the first time he was here. That was why she was so happy.

She and Bryden left at about ten o'clock. As they turned on to the highway he said, 'Are you free tomorrow evening, Casey?'

Had she had ten dates, she would have cancelled every one. 'I was planning to clean the apartment. But I could be distracted from that,' she said jauntily.

'Jenny and Matthew are having a party, and would like you to come.'

Casey had not seen Jenny since last September. 'You'll be there, of course,' she said, more as statement than as question. 'Sure, I'll go. What time?'

'Any time after eight. She's calling it a dessert party, so don't eat too much for dinner...she's hired a catering firm known for their cheesecakes and tortes.'

'That'll be fun, I haven't been to a party in ages.'

'None with the estimable Douglas?'

'He's given up on me,' she said. Some time in May Douglas had dropped one of his rather ponderous hints about the change in their relationship once her apprenticeship was over; she had told him as kindly as she could that she did not want any changes, that she was content with the friendship they shared during working hours and wanted nothing more. He had been hurt, as she had known he would be, and she had hated causing him pain. But she had also known that Bryden was the man she wanted, and no other would do.

She could explain none of this to Bryden. She said, 'What should I wear tomorrow night?' and the conversation moved into safer channels.

When she pulled up in front of the Sibleys' house, Bryden said, 'Will you come in?'

'I'd better not—I have to be up at seven.'

He did not insist. 'Thanks for the drive, Casey. I'll see you tomorrow night,' he said, kissed her cheek with all the passion of a maiden aunt, and got out of the car with Bess. Casey watched until he had unlocked the front door. Then she drove off.

Bryden was looking for a new job in Ottawa. Did that mean he wanted to share more of his life with her?

* * *

At eight-thirty on Thursday evening Casey was ringing the doorbell of the big brick house where the Sibleys lived. Her white silk blouse, brief green leather skirt and patterned tights made her look slender and leggy and provocative, a look which her hair, gathered in a demure green velvet bow at the nape of her neck, should have ameliorated and did not.

She had hoped that Bryden would open the door. But it was Matthew who ushered her in. 'Casey!' he said hospitably. 'How nice to see you again, do come in. Would you like to take your jacket upstairs, the room on the right? Then we'll get you a drink.'

The curved staircase had a partial view of the living-room, from which emanated the convivial hum of a party well under way. Short of standing part way up and staring, Casey could not see Bryden. She left her jacket on the bed in company with several others, all more expensive than hers, and checked her appearance in the bevelled mirror; her hair was smooth as satin, while her brilliant eyes and flushed cheeks scarcely needed the make-up she had so carefully applied. She took a couple of deep breaths and went downstairs.

Jenny, in a dress of royal blue Thai silk that co-existed rather edgily with her vivid red curls, was waiting for her at the bottom of the stairs. 'Matthew told me you'd arrived; I'm so *delighted* you could come. I'll introduce you to a few people, and then I'll get you a drink. How are you?'

She led Casey into the living-room, which was furnished with extreme eclecticism, yet had a haphazard charm. Bryden was taller than most; Casey still could not see him. Swallowing a panic that seemed out of all proportion—what did she expect, that he had gone back to Ragged Island?—she said with an attempt at casualness that would not have deceived a child, 'Isn't Bryden here?'

'He was meeting a couple of business acquaintances for dinner; he should be along soon,' Jenny said vaguely, her eyes searching the room. 'Ah, there's a couple you'd like to meet.' And she led Casey across the room to an older man and woman who appeared to be having an argument in front of the bookshelves. There was something tantalisingly familiar about the man. Wondering whom he resembled, Casey heard Jenny say, 'Cressida, Harold, I'd like you to meet a friend of Bryden's...Casey Landrigan. Casey is a guide-dog trainer at the school where Bryden got his dog. Casey, these are Bryden's parents, Cressida and Harold Moore.' She gave Casey the smile of a woman who had achieved her purpose. 'Tell me what you'd like to drink.'

Harold Moore was glaring dyspeptically at Casey. 'A double rum and Coke,' Casey said, and smiled at his wife.

But before she could say anything, Cressida Moore had draped her chiffon-clad sleeve over Casey's arm and, leaning forward as if Casey was deaf, was breathing, 'What miracles you must accomplish! To give the blind sight, to move them from a world of darkness and despair into the light of freedom, to guide their every step and teach them anew the glory of life...ah, if only I were younger, I could embrace such work with all my heart.'

Casey blinked, not sure how to respond to such a confusion of prejudice and misinformation. Cressida Moore's eyes, hedged with mascara, were swimming in sentimental tears that she began dabbing at ineffectually with a lace-bordered handkerchief. Casey said carefully, 'I don't think——'

'You're too modest, my dear, too modest.' Cressida's voice had a tremolo worthy of any soprano. 'Your task is so admirable—giving the blind the appearance of normality. So they seem the same as the rest of us.'

'Those who have lost their sight are normal in every respect but that——' Casey began, her eyes blazing.

But Harold Moore interrupted. 'Far too much fuss being made,' he snorted. 'A waste of the taxpayers' money.'

'The school operates almost entirely on donations,' Casey said pleasantly.

'Lot of hogwash. Bryden was managing fine without a dog.'

'But it's such a beautiful dog,' Cressida cried. 'Those big brown eyes...I don't know how you can bear to discipline the dogs, Miss Landry, if they're all as sweet as Bess.'

'Landrigan,' said Casey. 'A dog should always——'

'Sweet?' Harold Moore retorted. 'That's the problem with you, Cressida, you wear rose-tinted glasses. That dog is a semi-domesticated carnivore who happens to have been taught a few cute tricks. Bryden did not need a dog. It's just another way for him to gain attention and sympathy.'

Perhaps fortunately at this juncture a white-jacketed waiter brought Casey's drink on a silver tray. She took a hefty swallow and tried to change the subject. 'Do you live in Ottawa, Mr Moore?'

Cressida, whose cheeks were patched with hectic colour, snapped, 'Bryden needs a great deal of attention and sympathy, Harold! Far more than you're prepared to give him. It's been such a terrible tragedy for me, Miss Landry, quite terrible, to suddenly find myself the mother of a blind man, to have to watch him struggling to do the simple little things we take for granted, to see him helpless, an object of pity. My heart aches for him. My poor Bryden——'

Casey fought to control any number of emotions, the chief of which was fury. She said crisply, 'Bryden does not need pity, Mrs Moore. He is an extremely intelligent man who is using all his skills to surmount what is certainly a terrible deprivation, but by no means an end to what you call normal life. A guide-dog is just one aspect of his struggle. The dog gives him greater freedom of movement and increased independence. That's all. Bryden does the rest.'

'That's sweet of you, dear,' quavered Cressida, who plainly did not believe a word Casey had said.

'I'm sick to death of all this modern psychological claptrap,' Harold announced. 'In my day we kept a stiff upper lip and didn't expect the rest of the world to come running to our rescue. We were the captains of our souls, Miss Landrigan, we were the masters of our fates. None of this sloppy-minded, wishy-washy liberalism!'

He gave Casey a militant nod. He had eyes only a shade lighter than his son's, but they were protruberant in a choleric complexion. Casey, who had not been aware she had been expressing either claptrap or liberalism, gave him her most dazzling smile and said smoothly, 'I deal in practicalities, Mr Moore. A guide-dog enlarges Bryden's sphere of activity and enables him to move more easily within that sphere. Makes him, if you like, more the captain of his soul.'

'You know you've always hated dogs, Harold,' Cressida put in with real malevolence. 'The puppy Bryden had all those years ago—you had it shot.'

'And I'd do so again,' he said pompously. 'It was nothing but an ill-bred mongrel.'

'He loved it,' Cressida protested. 'It was an adorable little thing.'

'Given a free rein you would have made a sissy out of our son, Cressida—crying all over him every time he skinned his knee, allowing him to sleep with a flea-ridden mongrel, wanting him to go to the local school rather than the boarding school where my father and grandfather had gone. *I* went away to school when I was six.

No reason why he should not.' He drew himself up to his full height. 'I chose to make a man of him.'

Casey, with some effort, had managed to keep her face expressionless during this tirade. She was beginning to understand much more clearly the forces that had shaped Bryden. Smothered by the shallow emotions of his mother, repelled by his father's rigidity: no wonder Bryden had trouble with love. His defence had been to become a loner, sufficient unto himself, and she was becoming increasingly sure that she was the first woman to storm those defences.

Cressida tossed back her drink and said spitefully, 'Well, darling, you succeeded—Bryden's twice the man you are.' Her eyes filled with easy tears. 'Or he was, before that dreadful accident ruined his life. Because what kind of a future does he face? He'll be all alone. No woman in her right mind will look at him now.'

Casey said clearly, 'I consider myself to be in my right mind, Mrs Moore, and I find your son the most attractive man I have ever met.'

'*Darling!*' Cressida Moore gushed. 'We were just talking about you.'

Casey nearly dropped her glass. Knowing exactly whom she was going to see, she turned around. Bryden, looking exceedingly handsome in a three-piece suit, was standing a foot away from her. 'Good evening, Bryden,' she said with immense dignity.

He rested one hand on her shoulder and kissed her unhurriedly on the cheek. 'I thought eavesdroppers were supposed to hear only ill of themselves.'

'She probably feels sorry for you, darling,' said his mother.

Casey's breath hissed between her teeth. Imperturbably Bryden remarked, 'Hello, Mother. No, she doesn't feel sorry for me. We had that one out several months ago.'

'Oh? So you've known each other quite a while?'

'September,' Casey said, with a brevity that probably sounded rude and for which she did not apologise.

With a puzzled frown, as if Casey had just admitted to an unmentionable disease, Cressida said, 'How strange! You're a very lovely young woman...but I suppose because you work with blind people all the time, it doesn't bother you being around Bryden.' She gave an affected little shudder. 'I'm terribly sensitive, you see, so I feel things more than the average person.' Then she turned to Bryden and cried, 'Oh, darling, I've done it again—why do I use words like see and look around you? I'm so sorry, I don't mean to be cruel!'

Casey had never met anyone with such a gift for un-intended insult. Before Bryden could respond, she said strongly, 'I enjoy Bryden's company, that's why I choose to be with him.' And the only reason he bothers me is because I want to take him to bed, she thought, wishing for Bryden's sake she could say it out loud.

'I suppose he's like an extension of your job,' Cressida said kindly.

'We've had that one out too, Mother,' Bryden remarked.

Frantically Casey searched for something to say. 'We've strayed rather a long way from guide-dogs, haven't we?' she managed. 'You should visit our school, Mr Moore, you'd probably find it very interesting.'

Pointedly Harold Moore looked all around Bryden's feet. 'And where is this wonder dog? Don't tell me you can get along without it.'

'Bess is upstairs—she'd be in the way in a crowded room like this,' Bryden replied with praiseworthy re-straint. 'How did your deal go with the computer company on Monday?'

'Now, Bryden, you know I dislike talking business in front of your mother,' Harold said huffily. 'Although actually I do have to admit it was finalised very much to my advantage.' He preened his moustache. 'It's a good thing I'm making some money—you seem to show no signs of going back to work.'

Casey saw Bryden's jaw tighten, and knew she had had enough. She took his hand and pressed it between her arm and her body, hoping he could feel the swell of her breast, and said limpidly, 'Will you excuse both of us? Some friends of ours have just arrived...it's been so nice meeting you.'

Informative would have been a more accurate word than nice, she thought, as she led Bryden away. So much for her much-vaunted honesty. Then Bryden said in a low voice, 'What friends?'

'The Drapers. Whose cottage began all this.'

'As long as you still consider them friends...by the way, you might want to lower my hand by six inches. Unless you're trying to drive me mad with lust in the middle of this rather sedate party.'

'I wanted to take your mind off your parents,' Casey retorted. 'Whom you and Jenny engineered that I meet. You're shutting me out again, Bryden.'

'If we're going to have a fight, I suggest we do it somewhere other than in front of the Drapers.'

'In that case I'll save it until later,' Casey promised. Then she donned a bright social smile. 'Hello, Susan, how are you?'

The party continued. The desserts were both delicious and calorie-laden, and, having disposed of rather more than her share, Casey found herself and Bryden temporarily separated from the rest of the crowd. She said, 'Why don't we disappear for a few minutes—no one will miss us.'

'There's a sun-room leading off the kitchen.'

The caterers were in efficient control of the kitchen. Casey complimented the chef on the hazelnut torte before

leading the way into the solarium and closing the door.
She let out her breath in a long sigh, tried to wriggle the
tension from her neck and said, 'What wonderful
plants!'

A profusion of hibiscus, amaryllis and begonias
flaunted their showy blossoms in every corner. 'We didn't
come here to admire the plants, Casey,' Bryden said drily.
'We came to have a fight.'

She glowered at him. 'This evening was another set-
up, wasn't it? You wanted me to meet your parents and
you didn't want to be around when I did.'

He made no attempt at denial. 'Jenny wasn't respon-
sible this time, though—I was the one who suggested it.
She just helped out.'

'With something less than subtlety.' Casey added
carefully, 'Are you trying to warn me off?'

His face guarded, he said, 'My parents go along with
me, Casey... and they're a far cry from yours.'

She thought of the love and support that had surrounded her since she was a baby, and which she had
tended to take for granted, and said frankly, 'You must
have had the personality of an ox not to have been driven
mad by the age of two.'

He said with a faint smile, 'I took the coward's way
out—I ran away. Only the place I ran was inside myself,
where they couldn't touch me.'

'It's called survival, not cowardice,' Casey said shortly.
'Did you think *I'd* run away once I'd met your parents?
That they'd scare me off?'

'I wanted you to be free to run if you so chose,' he
said in a tight voice.

'I'm still here,' she said quietly.

'They made me what I am,' he said, slamming one
fist against the other with a violence that made her jump.
'It's only since I met you that I've understood I don't
have to stay that way for the rest of my days—that love

and happiness can be mine in a way I never thought possible. You're so alive, Casey, so overflowing with warmth and generosity and laughter...'

'You can trust me,' she whispered. 'I won't go away.'

He brought a hand up to her cheek. 'Promise?'

'Promise,' she said, and all her love was in the single word.

As he found her mouth and kissed her with fierce dedication, cupping her face in his hands, she rested her palms against his chest, feeling the heat of his skin seep through his shirt, searching for the heavy beat of his heart. Between short, hard kisses he was muttering her name. His hands drifted down her throat, his fingertips as delicate as the brush of feathers on her flesh. Then he traced the rise of her breast under the silk fabric.

She swayed towards him, pliant as the pine boughs in the sea winds at the cottage. He said hoarsely, 'I won't rest until I have you in my bed. I——'

Light streamed into the room and Jenny said, 'This is the solarium, which we only finished a year ago...oh, I didn't know anyone was in here.'

Casey sprang away from Bryden, her cheeks as red as the hibiscus that nodded at her side. 'We were just leaving,' she babbled.

Bryden said with considerable panache, 'Casey has been admiring your green thumb, Jenny.'

Whatever Casey had been admiring had been quite unrelated to any part of Jenny. She said valiantly, 'That pink and white amaryllis is absolutely gorgeous.'

'Isn't it?' Jenny said complacently. She introduced the couple that was with her, whose names Casey could never afterwards recall, and somehow Casey contributed with reasonable intelligence to a discussion on the care of tropical blooms. Then they all joined the party in the living-room again, where she had a cup of very strong coffee. When she had finished it, she said, 'Bryden, I've got to go, I have to work tomorrow.'

They were near the front door, surrounded by people whose noise level indicated a very successful party. Bryden said, 'Can I call you at work tomorrow morning when I hear about the job?'

'Of course!'

In the same even voice he said, 'Thanks for not running away.'

Someone bumped into her and apologised profusely. 'I'll never do that,' Casey vowed.

'Just remember that I want you more than I have ever wanted anything or anyone in my entire life.'

She wanted to kiss him; she wanted to cry. As two more people jostled her, she said acerbically, 'You do choose your moments, Bryden Moore.'

'I'll learn to do better in the future...did you have a coat?'

'Upstairs.'

'I'll wait for you here.'

Her jacket was submerged under a mound of suede. Casey threw it round her shoulders and ran downstairs. Bryden was talking to Matthew and Jenny; she thanked them for a lovely party, kissed Bryden full on the mouth, and left.

CHAPTER ELEVEN

At a quarter to ten the next morning Casey was loading a Labrador retriever into the van when Charlene, who managed the kennels, called through the window, 'Telephone, Casey!'

Casey latched the cage, climbed down from the van, and ran for the telephone, which was located outside the feed-room near the long row of pens. The three nearest dogs started to bark. 'Hello?' she gasped.

'This is Professor Bryden Moore speaking, of the mathematics department of Carleton University.'

'Bryden, you got the job!' she said warmly. 'I'm so happy for you, congratulations.'

'I'll have to acquire an air of absent-mindedness and a tweed jacket with leather elbow patches,' he joked. 'But before I do that, I'm planning a kidnapping...what the devil's that noise?'

'I'm in the kennels. Who do you want to kidnap?'

'You, of course.'

She tried to erase the silly grin from her face and said succinctly, 'When and why?'

'Five-fifteen at the airport. Bring enough old clothes for four days, plus that very sexy outfit you wore last night.'

She had not told Bryden or her parents that she had Monday and Tuesday off. 'How do you know I don't have to be back to work until Wednesday?' she demanded.

'David Canning told me. Two weeks ago.'

She scowled into the phone and said, 'Come clean, Bryden.'

'You're a very strong-willed woman,' he said plaintively. 'Not to say bossy. Maybe I should reconsider.'

'You're too late—I accept. Now tell me why you were talking to my boss.'

'With all due respect to your professional ethics, I felt eight years was too long to wait. Because what if I then wanted another dog? That would be another eight years. So I decided—are you listening, Casey?'

Wait for what? she wondered, in a turmoil of hope and panic. She said, only half joking, 'You're taking a very long time to get to the point.'

'I told David Canning my intentions towards you were highly honourable, that I was doing my best to get a job in Ottawa, and that our student-instructor role was not advancing my cause...what did you say, Casey?'

'N-nothing,' she spluttered.

'He was most sympathetic,' Bryden said blandly. 'From now on if there are any problems with Bess, I'll deal with Douglas rather than you. Which means we can be ourselves. Bryden and Casey.'

'I see,' Casey croaked.

'He also told me he was giving you a couple of days off after your exams, which he was quite sure you would pass with flying colours.' Abruptly Bryden dropped his bantering manner. 'That was when I took the risk of booking two seats to Halifax. Hoping that you would spend the four days with me at Ragged Island, Casey. But please don't think I took your answer for granted, because I didn't. *Will* you go with me?'

'There's nothing I'd like better,' she said.

There was a small silence. 'Thank God. I thought of going somewhere closer so you wouldn't have to fly, but I have this quite irrational urge to go back to the place where we met. Could you be at the airport by four-thirty?'

'If I'm going to be at the airport at four-thirty I'll have to stop talking on the phone—I've got a million things to do!'

'I'll meet you at the Air Canada ticket counter. Goodbye, Casey.'

He had rung off. She replaced the receiver and in a daze walked past the pens to get the other dog she would be working with that morning. She had asked Bryden why he was kidnapping her and he had not answered. Did honourable intentions mean marriage? Or was that only in Victorian novels? And would she and Bryden be sharing the big bed in his room? She remembered the heaped-up cushions whose colours glowed like jewels and discovered she was trembling.

But dawdling in the kennels would not answer any of her questions. Nor would it get her to the airport on time.

She must simply wait and see.

As it turned out, Casey had very little time to think about Bryden's proposal, honourable or otherwise. Brutus, the second dog she worked with that morning, seemed bent on breaking every rule of his training in the space of an hour. He gobbled some popcorn that had been spilled on the pavement, he tried to tree a big grey squirrel, and he hauled Casey halfway across the pavement when he sighted a black cat washing itself on a fence. With all the patience at her command Casey took him through his paces again and again until she was sure he was getting the message; which meant she was late for lunch and did not have the time to go to her apartment as she had hoped.

She worked with two other dogs that afternoon, both of whom behaved perfectly. At three-thirty she unloaded them from the van and ran the keys inside. David

Canning was crossing the hall. 'Haven't you left yet?' he demanded.

She considered a number of replies, shook her head and blushed.

'Off you go. And I don't want to see you before Wednesday morning.' His glasses slid a little further down his nose. 'Although I do expect an invitation to the wedding.'

'I haven't been asked to marry anyone yet,' Casey said.

'I'm sure you will be.' He waved her towards the door. 'Off with you!'

Casey had hoped to have time for a leisurely soak in the tub with lots of her favourite bath oil; instead she threw the bath oil in her travelling kit along with her other toilet articles. Jeans, sweaters, socks, shorts... mentally she ticked things off one by one, meanwhile carefully folding her white silk blouse in tissue paper and leaving the leather skirt to lie on top of everything else. She opened her lingerie drawer, packed her prettiest underwear and, after hesitating for a moment, added a nightdress her sister Anne had bought her a year ago: the kind of nightdress one wore on one's honeymoon. Then she changed out of her work clothes into a green three-piece linen suit whose loose, casual lines were very becoming.

It was ten minutes past four and it took twenty-five minutes to drive to the airport. She grabbed her suitcase, locked the apartment and ran down the stairs.

Half the population of Ottawa also seemed to be heading to the airport. There were delays at every traffic light and much of Casey's view was blocked by the transport truck that was ahead of her. The hand on her watch crept slowly towards the thirty-minute mark.

At twenty to five she drove into the car park, where she spent five minutes crawling along the lanes searching for an empty spot. She glimpsed one two lanes over, but by the time she got there it had been taken by a big black Cadillac. Then she saw another only three spaces away. She drove in and turned off the ignition.

The vehicle ahead of her, a flashy yellow sports car that had been backed into its space, was just leaving. The driver, who was young and male, gunned the motor and gave her a cheerful wave; too late she saw that his reverse lights were still on. She had time to brace herself before he reversed into the front of her car.

He leaped out, full of apologies and, when she got out of the car in her smart green suit, of admiration. The damage to her bumper was such that they had to exchange names; he would, she was sure, have asked her for a date if she had not said with frantic truth, 'I'm going to miss my plane—I've got to go!'

Grabbing her bag, she ran across the tarmac in her high heels; and in one of those sudden tricks of memory realised she had left her leather skirt hanging in the wardrobe. All she needed now, she thought desperately as the automatic doors swung open to admit her, was for Bryden to have gone on without her.

It was one minute after five. She searched the length of the Air Canada counters and saw him standing under the first class signs with Bess lying at his feet. His face was set in grim lines. Her heels clicking on the floor, she ran towards him.

'Bryden, I'm sorry!' she gasped. 'Everything's gone wrong from the minute you phoned. Have we missed the plane?'

He said harshly, 'I thought you'd changed your mind.'

'I told you I'd never do that. *I* was afraid you'd have gone on without me.'

'No fear of that, Casey.' Roughly he took her in his arms, expressing in his kiss all his pent-up fear and frustration.

The ticket agent said courteously, 'They're boarding your flight now, sir. You should proceed to gate twenty-one.'

'First things first,' Bryden growled and kissed Casey again.

They were the last passengers to get on board; by the time they were settled in their seats, the plane was taxiing away from the terminal. Casey was busy rattling off the disasters of her day; she reached the admiring young man in the yellow sports car just as they took off, and somehow managed not to mind the lift-off as much as usual. 'So that's why I was late,' she finished in a rush, releasing her clutch on Bryden's sleeve.

The aircraft was levelling off. She had survived again.

'It was the longest thirty minutes of my life,' Bryden said. 'But, in view of all you've told me, you're forgiven.'

As the steward brought them drinks, Casey requested, 'Tell me more about your job.'

He grinned boyishly. 'I'll be teaching mathematics to postgraduates and co-ordinating several research projects. So it's a big change from my other job, which was pure research and where I worked almost totally alone. This one involves a lot of contact with students and other professors.'

'You're coming out of the closet,' she said slowly.

'One of the reasons I holed up at Ragged Island was so I could work on the computer and find out what my limitations were.'

'I wasn't referring to your blindness,' Casey said even more slowly. 'I meant in terms of other people.'

'I can't fool you, can I, Casey? Of course that's at the root of the change—I want a job where I deal with people.'

'You won't be a lone wolf any more.'

He gave her a crooked grin. 'I never was much of a wolf.'

The pilot's voice came over the intercom, mentioning the cruising height and speed and describing the Nova Scotia weather as mild with coastal fog. Casey was so busy listening to Bryden's impressions of the university that she paid little attention to the weather; although the Halifax airport was wreathed in fog when they arrived there an hour later, the pilot made a faultless landing.

While she waited for the luggage Bryden took Bess for a walk; perhaps because she had been so late arriving at the airport in Ottawa, her suitcase was not among the baggage spewed on to the carousel. With a resigned sigh she went to the counter and entered a claim for it, and was told by the bored middle-aged clerk that it would be delivered the next morning. Then she and Bryden picked up the rental car, bought some groceries in the outskirts of Halifax and had a quick meal in a little restaurant in Bedford.

When they finally set off for Ragged Island it was dark, the fog thick enough that Casey had to concentrate on the guide line along the shoulder to keep herself on the road. Leaning forward in her seat, her hands gripping the wheel, she strained to penetrate the thick curls of mist. Bryden wisely kept silent, although he did say once, his voice full of frustration, 'This is when I hate being blind—everything falls on you.'

In this instance, at least, he was right. Casey said briefly, 'We should be there in half an hour.'

But as they got nearer to the sea the fog worsened, the headlights making such a small circle of yellow light that she was forced to drive even slower. So it was midnight before she turned into Bryden's driveway between the cedar hedges. She coasted down to the door, turned off the ignition and said with heartfelt relief, 'We're here. Thank goodness!'

'Let's get the stuff inside,' Bryden said shortly.

They unloaded groceries and suitcases and turned on the furnace to take the dampness from the house. Wishing she could dispel the tension in the air as easily, Casey said, 'Tea, cocoa, or a Scotch on the rocks?'

Bryden put his hand on her shoulder; it was the first time he had touched her since the airport in Ottawa. 'You've had a long day, Casey,' he said. 'You must be worn out. Why don't you go to bed...the last time the cleaning woman was here she made up the bed in the spare room. I'm going to take Bess for a walk on the beach, she's been cooped up all day and I need to stretch my legs as well.'

Nonplussed, Casey stared up at him. Although it had been a very long day and she was tired, she would have liked to walk on the beach in the fog; but she had not been invited. And from the first part of his speech, it looked as though Bryden's intentions were nothing if not honourable. In fact, she thought painfully, he looked as if he could not be rid of her soon enough.

Bess had heard her name and was sitting expectantly, her tail swishing on the pine floor. Bryden added with a reasonableness that Casey found intensely irritating, 'After all, you're here for four days, we've got lots of time.'

Time for what? she wondered, watching him take Bess's collar out of his kit bag. Not sure she could trust her voice, she said flatly, 'Have a nice walk,' and headed for the stairs.

Under other circumstances Casey would have been delighted to stay in the guest bedroom with its attractive rock maple furniture and peach-coloured carpet. But she had passed beyond tiredness to a kind of hyper-sensitivity, her nerves twitching, her brain racing, her eyelids scratchy. She kicked off her shoes, childishly pleased with the thunk they made as they hit the wall. Had she put up with balky dogs, forgotten skirts,

crumpled bumpers and smooth-voiced pilots just to be
sent to bed like a naughty child?

She marched downstairs. Bryden and Bess had gone.

How dared he leave her alone? she thought venge-
fully. Dragging her all the way from Ontario to sleep in
the spare room...it was intolerable! If he was that much
of a loner, he'd got the wrong woman. And she was
going down to the beach right now to tell him so.

She stormed through the kitchen to the back porch,
where she pulled on an old raincoat and a pair of
Bryden's rubber boots and let herself out of the side
door, slamming it shut behind her. The mist, redolent
of the salt tang of the sea, bathed her face in coolness.
The boom of the foghorn sounded very close. She stalked
round the house to the back lawn and crossed it in the
light from the living-room windows.

Bryden's boots were far too big for her, and her hands
were lost in the sleeves of his coat. Clomping along,
Casey found the path into the woods, which gathered
her into their silent, damp darkness. In miniature rain-
showers drops fell from the boughs on to her face as the
foghorn, lonely voice of the sea, beckoned her forward.
Stoutly telling herself she could not possibly get lost,
Casey pushed onward. She could not go very fast, because of the boots; it was with a distinct feeling of relief
that she found the cedar steps to the beach.

The sand was damp, and even in the darkness she could
see the imprint of Bryden's steps and the miniature
craters where Bess had been running. The sigh of the
waves caressed her ears, and for a moment she forgot
that she was furious with Bryden. There was no wind
and the air was not cold; she let the boots fall from her
feet and stripped off her tights, leaving them at the foot
of the steps and wriggling her toes in the sand as she
headed purposefully towards the ocean.

The tide was low. There was a stretch of smooth, un-
marked sand, much cooler, then the wash of ice-cold
water over her bare feet. With a tiny shriek of dismay
Casey backed up.

The foghorn moaned through the mist. The white curl
of water advanced, retreated, advanced again, and suddenly she was aware of how the darkness and fog were
pressing in on her, encircling her, surrounding her. The
house could have been a thousand miles away, and she
the only person in the world . . . attacked by a paralysing
loneliness of spirit, she felt the last vestige of her anger
slip away like a retreating wave, and fear advance in its
place.

Bryden had left the house without her. Instead of
gathering her into his arms and making love to her, he
had sent her to the spare room and gone for a walk alone.
His parents have won, she thought in utter terror. Sure,
he had a new job and he was running in marathons and
getting his life in order after the loss of his sight. But
he was still afraid to love. Harold and Cressida had won.
She, Casey, had lost.

She shoved the back of her hand against her mouth
to prevent herself from crying out, whirled, and staggered across the sand. The foghorn pursued her, mocking
her, and she ran faster, wanting only the comfort and
security of the house.

Her foot struck a rock. She stopped dead, and felt
panic add itself to loneliness and pain, for as she peered
through the mist she saw the humped shapes of boulders,
and knew she had run towards the headland instead of
the steps. Behind her the waves sucked and gurgled
among the rocks, long strands of seaweed stirring lazily
in the water like the hair of the drowned. Her skin
crawled. She screamed Bryden's name into the darkness.

The fog smothered the sound of her voice. 'Bryden!'
she cried again, but only the hollow boom of the foghorn

answered her. He had vanished, she thought with another pang of terror. Insubstantial as the mist, he had gone from her life.

Thrusting her cold hands in her pockets, she tried to calm the battering of her heart against her ribs. Maybe this was a nightmare, like the ones she had had all last winter, and any minute she would wake and find herself in the maple bed in the spare room...

Then, like a nightmare, she heard something behind her, something that was not the splash of the waves. Frozen to the spot, straining her eyes, she glimpsed a dark shape emerging from the mist and gave a whimper of dread.

Bess barked. Bryden's voice said, 'Casey—is that you?'

Her body sagged. She stumbled towards him and threw herself into his arms, sobbing his name over and over again, burrowing her face into the wet nylon of his jacket. Bryden's arms went hard around her and he said, 'Thank God I've found you!'

As Bess sniffed at her bare ankles, his words penetrated her distress. 'What do you mean? *You* weren't looking for *me*. It was the other way round.'

'I certainly was looking for you! Five minutes after I came down here I realised I'd been a damn fool to leave you alone. So I was heading back to the house as fast as I could when Bess found the boots at the foot of the steps. That's how I knew you were down here, too.'

Casey raised her chin, all her anger rushing back. 'You flatter yourself when you say you were a damn fool! After all I've gone through today, I do not appreciate being sent to bed like a seven-year-old. If you want to be a loner, Bryden Moore, you go ahead—but you can count me out. *I'm* getting the first flight back to Ottawa tomorrow morning.' She finished with a defiant sniff.

He seized her by the elbows. 'I don't want to be a loner any more——'

'You have a funny way of showing it.' Her voice shook. 'You wouldn't even take me to bed!'

'Sweetheart, I had the best of motives for that...I wanted everything to be right. It's the first time for you, and you were tired and tense...so I thought we should wait until tomorrow.'

She drew a deep, hiccupping breath. 'You might at least have asked me how I felt about it.'

'That's the conclusion I came to down here in the fog, that of course I should have asked you. I'd been guilty of shutting you out again, making decisions on my own the way I always have.'

'Oh,' Casey said. 'I thought you didn't want me. At all.'

'Nothing could be further from the truth. The reason I came down to the beach was to work off some of my—er—energy.'

She said in a small voice, 'That's the second time you've called me sweetheart.'

As the foghorn echoed through the mist, Bess sat down on the sand and began to scratch herself. Bryden said quietly, 'I called you that because I love you, Casey.'

'I—*what* did you say?'

'Darling Casey, I love you with all my heart.'

They were the words she had waited for for months, spoken with all the passion she could have wished. With a sigh of utter contentment she rested her cheek on his jacket. 'Thank goodness,' she said.

'Is that all you've got to say?'

'I'm happier than I've ever been in my life.'

'Casey,' he said urgently, 'do you love me?'

In genuine surprise she said, 'Of course I do—didn't you know that?'

'Five minutes ago you were going to get the first flight back to Ottawa. No, Casey, I did not know that.'

She wrapped her arms around him. 'Bryden, dearest Bryden, I love you. With all my heart and soul I love you.' Then she reached up and kissed him.

He kissed her back with love and pent-up desire and with deep joy. 'I think we should go up to the house,' he said.

'Bess is getting wet and my feet are cold,' she said agreeably, taking his arm as the three of them walked across the sand. At the foot of the steps she put on his boots again, and together they threaded their way through the dark trees and across the lawn. She hung up her borrowed jacket in the back porch; by now she was feeling both shy and frightened, for she had never made love before and had no idea how they were to make the transition from the cluttered porch to the bedroom.

As if he sensed her diffidence, Bryden said easily, 'Do you want a quick shower to get rid of the sand, Casey? I'll lock up.'

'OK,' she mumbled and fled for the stairs.

The shower got rid of the sand and warmed her feet, although it did nothing for her nervousness. Her seductive nightgown, which might have helped, was in her suitcase somewhere between Ottawa and Halifax; she pulled on a robe of Bryden's that was hanging on the bathroom door and padded into the hall. Bryden's door was ajar.

The carpet muffling her footsteps, she crossed the hall and edged around his door. Although the covers had been pulled back, the bed was empty. Bryden was standing by the window; through an open louvre wafted the quiet rhythm of the waves. He was naked.

For a moment she gazed at him in simple pleasure, for the planes of his body from the broad shoulders and narrow hips to the long, lean legs were very beautiful to her. Then, with an ache in her heart, she wished fervently that he could see her as she was now seeing him.

He could not. He would never be able to.

But the desire that throbbed in her veins and dispelled her nervousness by its very insistence also told her what to do: she walked into his room, shedding the robe so that it fell in a tiny swish of sound to the floor. 'Bryden?' she whispered.

He had heard the soft fall of her steps. His body swung round. 'Come here, sweetheart.'

She walked right up to him, slid her arms up his hair-rough chest and kissed him. His hands went out to her; she felt the shock run through him as he discovered she also was naked. He groaned deep in his throat and pulled her against the length of his body.

When she felt the warmth and hardness, the muscle and bone that were the essence of him, the last of her fears vanished, for Bryden wanted her as passionately as she wanted him. The sound of the waves receded as they clung to each other, mouths devouring, hands frantically searching. Then he swung her into his arms and carried her over to the bed, laying her on her back, falling on top of her in his haste.

Glorying in his weight, Casey laced her fingers in his hair and kissed him again, their tongues dancing, their lips hungry for more. He rained kisses on her face, her throat, the soft hollows beneath her collarbones; he found the firm, ivory swell of her breast and traced it to its tip.

An arrow of sweetness pierced her to the core. Immersed in sensations new to her, utterly over-whelming in their intensity, Casey heard his hoarse whisper from a long way away. 'Casey, I love you. I love you so much, I can never have enough of you . . . tell me you'll marry me.'

She raised herself on one elbow, clutching his smooth, bare shoulder. 'Are you sure you want to marry me? Marriage is the opposite of being alone.'

He reached up and kissed her, then murmured against her mouth, 'More sure than I've ever been of anything in my life.'

In the dim light she searched his features, finding tension and love equally mingled. Holding his head to her breast, she dropped her cheek to his silky hair and cried joyfully, 'Yes...oh, yes. Because I love you so much.'

'I never thought I'd hear you say those words.'

'I've been wanting to say them for months. I was so afraid your parents would win, Bryden, that you'd stay a loner for the rest of your days.'

He eased her down on the pillows. 'How could I, when you've taught me how to share? Casey, I'll never shut you out again, I swear.'

With complete trust she opened her arms to him and whispered, 'Show me how much you love me, Bryden.'

He began caressing her with slow, sensual movements, seeking out one by one the places where she had never been touched before, and not until she was whimpering with pleasure and begging for more did he enter her. She felt no pain, only wonderment and a driving hunger that broke the last of her restraint. Through the gathering storm they travelled together, and together were flung into the waves and the wind's cry and the rhythms that could not be denied, and there Casey found the wild creature that Bryden had always made of her and joined that creature to him, woman to his man.

They were silent for a long time afterwards, resting in the storm's aftermath. Finally Casey said softly, running her finger along his upper lip, 'Thank you—that was wonderful.'

'For me, too.' He drew a strand of her hair gently through his fingers. 'I have the rest of my life to learn what you look like. To picture your beauty in my mind...to hold your love in my soul.'

It was not the first time Bryden had almost reduced her to tears. She nuzzled her face into his shoulder. 'I'm so glad we came here, where it all began.'

'I fell in love with you here.'

'You were very rude to me here!'

'That was because you scared me to death and entranced me at one and the same time. Little wonder that I tried to get rid of you.'

'I'm glad you didn't succeed,' Casey said with a contented sigh, threading her fingers through the hair on his chest.

'I'm glad I didn't, too.' He stroked the curve of her hip. 'And we have four more days...maybe we should spend them in bed, Casey.'

She gave a rich chuckle. 'Until my suitcase arrives, I don't have any proper clothes.'

'Fate,' he said solemnly. 'In the guise of an airline.'

Certainly, when a taxi delivered Casey's luggage at noon the next day, she and Bryden were still in bed.

This February,
Harlequin helps you
celebrate the most
romantic day of the
year with

my Valentine

1991

Katherine Arthur
Debbie Macomber
Leigh Michaels
Peggy Nicholson

A collection of four tender
love stories written by
celebrated Harlequin
authors.

Available wherever Harlequin books are sold.

VAL

COMING IN 1991 FROM
HARLEQUIN SUPERROMANCE:

THE·BYRNSIDE·INHERITANCE

1

Three abandoned orphans,
one missing heiress!

Dying millionaire Owen Byrnside receives an
anonymous letter informing him that twenty-six years
ago, his son, Christopher, fathered a daughter. The
infant was abandoned at a foundling home that
subsequently burned to the ground, destroying all
records. Three young women could be Owen's long-
lost granddaughter, and Owen is determined to track
down each of them! Read their stories in

#434 HIGH STAKES (available January 1991)
#438 DARK WATERS (available February 1991)
#442 BRIGHT SECRETS (available March 1991)

Three exciting stories of intrigue and romance by
veteran Superromance author Jane Silverwood.

Harlequin Presents®

Coming Next Month

Available in March wherever paperback books are sold, or through Harlequin Reader Service:

In the U.S.
P.O. Box 1397
Buffalo, N.Y.
14240-1397

In Canada
P.O. Box 603
Fort Erie, Ontario
L2A 5X3